Carl Lyons knew what was coming.

One of the technicians clamped alligator-jaw clips to Lyons's body. Another fastened a short strap across the Able Team specialist's forehead. Lyons could not move.

Then Dr. John, Unomundo's torture master, touched the button.

Lyons felt his body explode in a flash of yellow light. The pain was too intense to understand. Rivers of it flowed from his crotch to the top of his head; his body thrashed and twitched as he fell through a brilliant yellow universe.

Then it stopped....

Mack Bolan's

ABLE TEAM

ABLE TEAM
Death Strike

Dick Stivers

A GOLD EAGLE BOOK FROM
W🌐RLDWIDE

TORONTO · NEW YORK · LONDON · PARIS
AMSTERDAM · STOCKHOLM · HAMBURG
ATHENS · MILAN · TOKYO · SYDNEY

With special thanks to Mark Howell.

First edition December 1985

ISBN 0-373-61221-4

Special thanks and acknowledgment to G. H. Frost
for his contributions to this work.

Printed in Canada

1

Cold, predawn wind swept down from the Sierra de Cuchumatanes. Gadgets Schwarz and Rosario Blancanales cruised through the narrow streets of Huehuetenango, the provincial capital of the northwestern Departamento de Huehuetenango, Guatemala, searching for an address.

The two men of Able Team had received the phone call from Guatemala only hours before. Cryptic, short, spoken in broken Spanish, the message passed along by the teenage boy caller said only that Mr. Stone, the tourist, needed the help of his friends.

Gadgets and Blancanales had assembled a few items of equipment—radios, pistols, hiking gear—that they thought they could smuggle into Guatemala and took the next Air Force flight south. They had bribed a car-rental-agency employee to reopen the office at midnight. Then they drove north on the Pan American highway, high into the Guatemalan highlands, arriving before dawn as the small city awoke.

As they searched for the address the teenage caller had given them, they saw the local people rushing through the dark streets, hurrying to their work. Some huddled at bus stops, *indigenas* and *ladinos* in separate groups.

The *indigenas*—Mayans who still retained their culture and nationality despite four centuries of European slavery and exploitation—wore traditional black wool coats for warmth. *Indigena* men and women of the same pueblos stood together, *indigenas* of other pueblos and Mayan nations stood in others, separated by different customs and different languages.

The *ladinos*—Mayans who had abandoned their *costumbres* or Guatemalans of mixed race—wore polyester and nylon in imitation of modern fashions. But synthetic fabrics and zippered jackets offered no protection from the high-altitude winds. For shelter, the *ladinos* stood in corners, or stood with their backs to the wind, or sucked on cigarettes to numb themselves to the aching cold.

Blancanales looked for numbers on the fronts of the lavender, pink and blue stuccoed buildings. Some of the shops had signs or names, but few had numbers. When he saw a number, it read, 6-47.

"Six forty seven?" Blancanales wondered aloud. "Sixth Street, number forth seven?"

"Maybe Zone Six?" Gadgets suggested. "Remember that screwup in the capital? We had an address, but there were twenty-one different zones? For a total of twenty-one different addresses to check?"

"This city's too small for zones." Blancanales put his flashlight beam on the map. "The six means the cross street is Calle Sies—Sixth Street."

"But what's the street we're on?"

"There is the question.... Stop at the corner." Blancanales glanced at the confusion of advertisements and phone numbers painted around the doorway of a pharmacy. He waved his flashlight at one painted rectangle and saw a young man pointing an M-1 carbine. Blancanales raised both hands into view. "Put the car in neutral, Wizard. Then put both hands on the top of the steering wheel."

"What?"

"Just do it...and turn on the dome light."

When the interior light went on, the young guard left the doorway. His dark uniform of black boots, black pants, blue-black coat and black stocking cap had concealed him. Seeing the two unarmed North Americans in the car, he relaxed his hold on the M-1, raising the muzzle to point at the sky. He glanced across the street and gave a short whistle. A whistle answered.

Blancanales greeted the guard in Spanish and asked directions. Smiling, the young man pointed, saying, "Past the market, to the left, near the buses to the mountains." Then he returned to the darkness of the doorway.

Shifting into gear and accelerating, Gadgets sped away. "Thought all the soldiers down here wore camouflage."

"Didn't you read his shoulder patch?" Blancanales asked.

"Couldn't see."

"That wasn't a soldier."

"Then he was a serious security guard?"

"That was a police cadet."

"You mean, like a police explorer scout? They put cadets out all night with a rifle?"

"You saw it."

"And the Ironman came here for a vacation? When he could have gone to Hawaii? Too weird for words."

Slowing, Gadgets wove the rental car along a street lined with parked trucks and buses. Laborers carried boxes of vegetables on their backs, only a strap across each person's forehead to secure the loads. On the curbs, women knelt beside huge round baskets wrapped in rope netting. The women unwrapped the netting and padding of cloth to display their avocados, bananas and chickens. A sign over a double doorway identified the block-wide building as the municipal market.

To one side, Gadgets and Schwarz saw shops built into the side of the market. Some of the shops remained closed, others had opened for business. Inside, men hunched over tables, eating wadded tortillas and spooning down soup. In other shops, vendors prepared their displays of cloth, fertilizer or farm tools.

"There, left, this is the street." Blancanales told his partner.

The left turn took them along another side of the market. Gadgets braked as a porter carried a net-wrapped bag of flour in front of the car. They saw his eyes glance in their direction as he hurried past.

"That's a fifty-kilo bag! One hundred ten pounds—you think that guy himself weighs a hundred and ten? How can he do that? Carry that load?" Gadgets asked.

"Maybe he's got children who need to eat," Blancanales replied. "Go up there—the address will be two blocks ahead."

Passing trucks and crowds, they came to an area crowded with pushcart cafés. Cooks worked by gas lanterns to warm tortillas and ladle out steaming portions of soup. Workers in ragged clothes and *indigenas* in the *traje* of their pueblos stood at the carts, eating the soup from clay bowls, using tortillas to push the stew into their mouths. Blancanales pointed to a doorway that had a sign over it reading Hotel Papaguayo.

"What a pit." Gadgets commented. Bare electric bulbs illuminated rows of dirty sleeping cubicles. Dogs lay on the oily packed-earth courtyard. Rolling down his window, he grimaced. "What a smell! This is where our buddy comes to have a good time?"

"Wait here." Blancanales told him as stepped into the street.

"Oh, yeah. I'll wait here," Gadgets answered, talking out loud to himself. "You think maybe I'm going to go check out the girls at the pool? Maybe try to score at the hotel disco? Maybe I'll go surfing—"

"Señor Wizard?"

A woman leaned down to the car window. An *indigena*, she had the sharp features and softly Asiatic eyes of her people. A lifetime of work and worry had lined her face, making her appear middle-aged. She wore a dark wool blanket over her shoulders.

Gadgets recognized the brilliant purple and red cloth of her *huipile* before he recognized her. The first time he had seen her, he had lowered his rifle and she had taken that opportunity to aim a Colt Government Model .45 ACP at his chest.

"*Sí, Señora Juana. ¿Dónde está mi amigo Ironman?*"

Then Blancanales returned. He spoke with the Quichenera in slow Spanish, repeating her words and repeating himself several times to confirm the answers. Then he got in the car. Juana walked away quickly.

"Follow her. They're at another hotel. She's been waiting all night, watching to see who showed up."

"What goes with Lyons?"

"She doesn't know. She thinks the International got him."

"Oh, man!"

"Yeah. Question is, is he dead or alive?"

Juana hurried away from the crowds of the market. She walked quickly, her bare feet flashing beneath her ankle-length black skirt. She seemed oblivious to the stones and shattered glass littering the street. At the second street, she cut right, continued to another street, then cut left.

At idling speed, Blancanales and Gadgets rolled through the narrow streets, staying a few car lengths behind the Quichenera. She darted around another corner, into a street no wider than an alley.

"This is making my paranoia come alive," Gadgets commented. He pulled a cloth flight bag from under the seat and pulled back the long zipper.

"Go easy," Blancanales cautioned him. "The police look in that bag, we're in prison."

Ahead, they saw only an empty street. Gadgets continued on, his head whipping from side to side as he scanned the area. He drove with his left hand, his right hand inside the flight bag. Then Juana ran along side them, tapping on the window again. She pointed to herself and then inside the car. Blancanales leaned back and opened the rear passenger door.

She slid in, awkward with the unfamiliar vehicle, and Blancanales told her how to pull the door closed. She glanced back, watching the street behind them as she urged them on with hand gestures and strange guttural words.

"What's she saying?"

Blancanales spoke quickly with Juana. She switched to Spanish. Blancanales relayed her words to his partner. "Just go. Weave through the streets. She says they'll kill us all if they follow."

"Who?"

"Who do you think?"

The storefronts and steel rolling doors of the commercial district became the multicolored stucco walls of homes. Other cars rattled over the brick streets, swirls of dust hanging in the bluing dawn light. After watching the street behind them, Juana turned her attention to the rented car. She ran her hands over the vinyl upholstery, touched the trim details of plastic and chrome. She ran her hand over the curved glass of the side window. Gadgets watched her in the rearview mirror.

"What is this scene?" Gadgets asked, incredulous. "One minute, she's playing that Hitchcock heroine, next, she's making like this Nipponmobile is a Maserati. Hasn't she ever seen a car before?"

Blancanales translated the question. She answered in broken Spanish. She and the Puerto Rican warrior talked for a minute, then Blancanales translated for his partner.

"No. She hasn't. Not from the inside. Nate had an old pickup truck. She thought that was luxury. Before that, she'd only been in buses and cattle trucks."

Juana spoke again to Blancanales. Blancanales showed her the map of the city, but she shook her head and pointed back. "She says we should go back now."

"Go back to that market? Why'd we drive out here?"

"Their hotel is near the square."

"The square what?"

"The town square—" Blancanales held up the map. "Back here. To the west of the market. We passed it as we came in from the highway."

"Back we go." Gadgets returned the flight bag to concealment beneath his legs.

In two minutes, they came to a traffic signal. Brilliant slanting dawn light cut across the town. Motorcycles whined through the intersection, followed by a troop carrier crowded with standing soldiers in camo and field gear. Gadgets looked up, startled.

"There's a giant clamshell on that roof. Look at that...."

"A bandshell. Bands play there. Go two streets and go right."

"Yes, sir. No time to play tourist. Forget the weird."

Accelerating, Gadgets raced a motorcyclist past the square. He beat the next light, then whipped through a right turn and stood on the brakes to avoid hitting a man leading a mule loaded with un-painted chairs. The lightweight chairs hung on both sides of the mule and continued upward in a pyramid. Gadgets leaned out his window and looked up. The swaying load of chairs went to the height of the second-story windows overlooking the street. "Way weird...."

As they continued, Blancanales counted off the streets, then motioned for Gadgets to make a right turn. "It'll be just around the corner. You want to stay with the car?"

"No one else to do it." Gadgets parked the car and pulled out his flight bag. "I'm going to that café over there. Have a cup of coffee and a tortilla."

Blancanales took his own flight bag, and Juana led him around the corner. As she knocked at a steel door and waited, Blancanales looked back and saw Gadgets go to an open café and take a table. Blancanales gave the street of two-story shops and apartments a quick scan, glancing at the windows, the balconies overhanging the sidewalks, the rooflines. He saw nothing alarming. But would he recognize a threat if it existed?

Metal rattled, and a peephole door opened. A powdered and rough Caucasian face peered out at Juana, and a sneer formed on the gaudy red lips. The peephole squeaked shut. A dead bolt slammed open.

The fair-skinned but aged landlady pulled open the sheet-metal door. Her lip twisted into a sneer, and she stood at the side, glaring down at Juana. She greeted the *indigena* with a sarcastic, *"Buenas dias, señora. Pase adelante."*

But when she saw Blancanales—dapper in his sports coat and slacks, his well-cut hair, his expensive wristwatch, his Pan Am flight bag—her sneer turned into a broad welcoming smile. Blancanales could count every porcelain tooth in the upper and lower plates of her false teeth. Her wrinkled hand went to her dyed black hair.

"Oh, señor. Buenas dias."

In a flash of inspiration, Blancanales remembered the Quichenero words for greeting. He had spent a few days with Nate and his family and he still remembered a few words of their language. He nodded to the white-skinned woman and said: *"Chan xacwil."*

The landlady was visibly startled, and Blancanales passed without another glance.

Juana's bare feet slapped on the polished tiles as she led him to a back room next to the laundry sink. Knocking at the door, she turned and explained to Blancanales in her awkward Spanish. "She make us pay double; she treat us like dogs. But we need room here. We do what Mr. Stone tell us."

Marylena, Nate Beck's wife, opened the door with her baby in her arms. For the next half hour, Blancanales talked with the two women and Juana's teenage son Xagil. He learned what had happened in the previous days. But what had happened to his partner Carl Lyons—a.k.a. Ironman, a.k.a. Mr. Stone—remained unknown.

Blancanales left the hotel and crossed the street to join Gadgets at the café table.

"Nate's dead. Lyons is missing. He's either dead or captured. They don't know what."

"Oh, man...." Gadgets groaned.

Neither man spoke for a moment.

Finally, Gadgets said "So how do we find out?"

"Xagil will take us into the mountains. We'll find out for ourselves.

2

Sheep grazed on the rolling, grass-covered foot-hills. Swerving the rented car around the worst of the potholes, Gadgets maintained a speed of thirty-five miles per hour on the road. The road had been paved with asphalt, but traffic and weather had reduced stretches to rocky dirt. In the distance, the Cuchumatanes stood against the horizon.

Xagil rode in the back seat, listening to Latin pop music scratchy with static playing on the car radio. From time to time, he leaned forward over the front seat and spun the knob, searching for stations. Only one other station reached the AM band receiver, and it played the same disco and ballad records. Changing stations only changed announcers, though even their inane chattering was similar.

Finally, exasperated, Gadgets switched off the radio. He slipped a cassette in a portable stereo and pressed the play button. Kandian dance music, played with drums, sitars and flutes, accompanied by Singhalese singing, filled the interior of the car.

"What do you think of this music, kiddo?"

"No entiendo inglés...."

"What? You don't understand Singhalese? The beautiful language of Sri Lanka? Don't they teach Singhalese in school here?"

"Wizard, he said he didn't understand English."

"Not English, either! What's the world coming to...."

"*¡Una patrulla civil!*" Xagil pointed to a group of men standing at the side of the road. They wore the clothes of *ladinos*—ragged polyester pants, jackets and scuffed work boots. As a sign of their paramilitary authority, they also wore straw hats painted in camouflage patterns. A plastic blue and white Guatemalan flag flapped at the end of a long pole.

The men waved the foreigners to a stop with their old bolt-action rifles.

"No mirrors," Gadgets commented. "We won't have any problems here."

Rolling down their windows, the two North Americans looked out at the men manning the checkpoint. The *ladinos* commented to one another when they saw Xagil.

The patrol motioned them out of the car. Hands on the roof, Xagil and the *norteamericanos* submitted to a patdown search. Gadgets whistled along with the strange melody of the Kandian songs.

One man held out his hand and demanded their papers. Other men looked inside. Gadgets and Blancanales gave them their passports, and Xagil handed them his identity card.

As the leaders studied the United States passports, the others listened to the strange music and joked to one another. Gadgets said to Blancanales, "What're those dudes looking for in our passports? They can't read."

Blancanales glanced to the man examining his passport. Holding the blue booklet upside down, the *ladino* leafed through the pages, studying every entry and exit stamp. The pages had been marked with an assortment of stamps, showing travel in Europe and Central America, all forged. He opened the passport to the photo of Blancanales and glanced from the photo to the foreigner. Only when the man closed the book and saw the American eagle upside down did he turn the booklet upright.

The patrolmen motioned for Gadgets to open the trunk. Two men looked in at the luggage but did not open the suitcases.

A minute later, Gadgets was speeding away. "Those dudes better not look for work in Beirut. Didn't even search the trunk. Didn't look under the hood. Didn't—"

"Quiet, Wizard. Just drive."

"How they going to stop the international Cuban conspiracy if they don't look up the exhaust pipe? Fidel himself could've been up there, hiding behind his beard."

"Castro couldn't get up an exhaust pipe."

"Yeah, he's too fat."

Blancanales only shook his head at the nonsense. As they drove higher into the mountains, pines appeared on the ridgelines. Walls of volcanic stone enclosed stone houses. Rutted dirt roads and foot trails led away from the highway. They saw several of the poles with the blue and white plastic flags. At one trail, a group of civil patrolmen searched a woodcutter and his cordwood-loaded mule.

"Look up the mule's exhaust pipe!" Gadgets called out as they passed. "That's where Fidel is—"

"Quit it!"

"Just jiving, man."

"What if they jive back with their rifles?"

"Those antique Mausers? They get off one shot—"

"And that one shot could go through the car and me and you and keep going out to the horizon."

A half hour later, they came to a crossroad. A wide dirt road, paved with gravel and broken stone, led into the forest. At the side of the road, a Guatemalan flag fluttered on a pole. But no patrolmen manned the position. Gadgets honked the horn. Blancanales knocked his hand away from the wheel and pointed ahead. Gadgets grinned and accelerated up the grade.

Xagil looked out the windows, alternating from side to side, looking high above the road, searching the forested mountainsides with his eyes. The trees stopped abruptly a few hundred yards from the road. Hundreds of stumps showed that the forest had extended into the narrow valley at one time. Sheep grazed in the cleared areas.

Blancanales compared their surroundings to a topographical map. He glanced to the ridge, noted the curves of the road, then studied the map. Gadgets drove and bebopped to the incomprehensible South Asian music. As they went over a hill, Gadgets slammed on the brakes.

"Someone had a checkpoint here," he told Blancanales. Switching off the cassette, Gadgets pointed to a ridge beside the road. The ridge angled down the mountainside to the narrow flat strip of the valley, but was scarred where earth movers had cut through the slope.

Beer cans and candy wrappers indicated an all-day stay. Boots had flattened the dry, bristly grass of the surrounding hillsides. Lines of footsteps led to an observation post high on the mountainside.

"They hung out here all day long, watching the road," Gadgets continued. "Count the beer cans, divide by the number of different boots, and you'll know what time the soldiers quit yesterday."

Blancanales questioned Xagil in quick Spanish. Xagil nodded. He pointed to both sides of the road, counting out soldiers with his points.

"Confirmed," Blancanales agreed. "But nothing happened here. Xagil says they'd left Lyons hours before. They heard helicopters coming and going. And when he and the women passed here, the soldiers didn't even look at them. Soldiers didn't stop them or question them. Xagil says there were two men up the mountain with binoculars, watching the area."

Speaking with Xagil again, Blancanales showed the boy the map. The teenager looked at the map, looked at the mountains overlooking the narrow valley, then turned his head to look sideways at the whorls and lines.

Gadgets interrupted. "Quit it, Political. You're just confusing him. Not everyone went to Fort Benning."

Taking away the map, Blancanales questioned the boy and finally got an answer. He relayed the answer to Gadgets. "He said from here to where they came down the mountain, they walked part of the day. Maybe three hours.''

"That's the information I can process.'' Gadgets threw the car in gear and sprayed dust and gravel as he accelerated. He turned on the Singhalese tape. "Half hour by car. Don't let me pass the place.''

As the road snaked on, the mountainsides became steeper, to the point where the angles didn't allow the planting of corn. Only sheep tracks lined the grassy slopes. Sheer rock walls loomed over the road. Gadgets whipped the car from side to side, maneuvering past holes and jutting stones, swinging the small car past rockfalls.

Heavy trucks had passed recently. Tires had broken smaller stones, knocked others to the side.

The road left the valley floor and switchbacked across the mountainsides. As they entered the clouds, moments of wind-driven white hid the sun, creating moments of semidarkness. Gadgets struggled with the steering, fighting the lurching and heaving of the suspension to guide the front wheels through the rocks. He had to slow to a crawl. Then they rounded a curve and Xagil shouted in Spanish, "Here, here! We came down here!''

A slope led higher into the mountains. From the road, they saw clouds sweeping through rocks and dense forest, the contrasts of white against gray and deep, shadowed green, like images from classical Chinese landscapes. Brilliant blue sky provided the background for the scene.

"The Ironman always liked mountains,'' Gadgets commented. He searched for a place to park.

Talking with Xagil, studying the map, Blancanales determined where the group had left Lyons. He
plotted their path up the mountain. "Looks like it
will take hours to get up there—"

"But only a few minutes to get down," Gadgets
countered. "Quicker if we had parachutes. Or hang
gliders. We leave everything lethal here?"

"We'll take radios and pocket knives. We could
say we don't know about the radio law. But full-
auto pistols and grenades? No...."

Gadgets stood at the side of the road, gazing up
at the forest. "Anything in the world could be up
there."

"Maybe even Carl," Blancanales added.

"Maybe...." Reaching under the car, Gadgets
got out their gear. He kept only their secure-
frequency hand radios, returning their Beretta 93-
R silenced pistols, their MU-50G controlled-effect
grenades and the radio-triggered C-4 charges to the
plastic cases and resecured the cases to the under-
carriage of the car.

With radios and water in their day packs, they
went up the hill. Xagil found his own sandal prints
and followed the route he and the women had taken
coming down the mountain. The extreme angles of
the mountainside often forced him to abandon the
route and zigzag up the slopes, crossing and re-
crossing his tracks. Despite their years, Blancanales and Gadgets kept up with the teenager, their
off-mission physical-conditioning discipline pay-
ing off in the high altitude.

The day alternated between hot and chill, hot
when the sun shone on their backs, chill when
clouds swept over them. The pines provided relief

from the sun and wind, but the clouds curled through the forest. From time to time, the density of the cloud fog forced them to walk only a few steps apart. They watched the gray form of Xagil ahead of them and kept moving through the mist.

Xagil finally stopped. He searched through the weeds and ferns, then turned over a rock. They saw a few bits of trash: a wad of paper, dirt-encrusted adhesive tape, a discarded rag that had been a baby's diaper. The teenager explained the trash to Blancanales.

"He says this is theirs," Blancanales translated to his partner. "Lyons took everything that could have alerted the soldiers and packed it all away. This is what he missed. He figured that if Xagil and the woman had anything from an American, the soldiers might ask where the American was. This means we're close."

"Got it."

They spread out on the slope and zigzagged through the forest, searching. Near-vertical sections forced them to bear south. Blancanales found tracks immediately. He keyed his hand-radio and said, "Big boots...civilian boots."

Gadgets acknowledged with quick clicks and kept searching. Blancanales followed the prints upward. Despite the extremely steep slope and the weight of his weapons and pack, Lyons had gone straight up the mountain. Blancanales saw where his partner had used the steel butt of a Galil rifle to claw his way up the slope.

As they approached the ridgeline, the Americans moved slowly, silently. Blancanales gave Xagil a hand signal to stay low, then went flat in the grass and ferns. He crept forward slowly, pushing the weeds aside, only his eyes and forehead showing as he bellied up the last few yards.

Nothing moved on the ridge. He heard the wind rushing through the pines, the sounds of birds. Trees swayed and branches creaked against one another. He scanned the area, squinting against glare, straining to see into the shadows. But he saw only forest and rocks. He put his hand-radio to his lips and whispered, "Wizard, stay low for a few minutes. Let's just watch, see if anything moves—"

But Xagil broke the silence. He rose from a tangle of grasses and walked to the ridge crest. The crunching of branches and dry leaves alarmed the birds. The songs stopped. Xagil walked through the forest, looking for the two Americans. Gadgets buzzed his partner. "The kid thinks it's cool...."

Xagil stopped. He picked up something. Sunlight flashed from what he held. Then he whistled with it.

Returning his hand-radio to his day pack, Blancanales went to the teenager. Xagil signaled again, three clear whistle tones. Seeing Blancanales, he held out the object.

It was a cartridge casing, a 5.56 mm.

Looking over the area, Blancanales saw areas of trampled-down grass and brush. Dirt held the prints of boots.

"Over here, Pol," Gadgets called out.

Flies buzzed around a vast scab of blood. Ants worked at the hardened slab. Gadgets squatted near it, lining up the angle of fire from where Xagil had found the cartridge casing.

"Seems like they were looking for him," Gadgets commented. "Got him surrounded. Then he ambushed them."

"There's got to be more here." Blancanales jogged back to where Lyons had fired from concealment. He found the marks of Lyons sliding through the bush.

All through the day they searched, finding cartridge casings, bandages, trash from markets in the capital. But they did not find Carl Lyons.

Finally they returned to the parked rented car.

"They got him," Gadgets concluded. "Alive or dead, they got him.

3

Darkness and pain.

Sensations. Lyons saw shapes and designs moving within the darkness, patterns of somber luminous colors swirling through the absolute black within his eyes. He felt and heard a vibration, a steady droning sensation and sound unrelated to the smashing of his pulse within his skull. He tasted plastic and realized they had immobilized his jaws with a strap. But one sensation dominated his returning consciousness....

Pain. Pain held him in a rigid seizure of dread. He could not summon the courage to move. Every surge of blood through his arteries, every breath swelling his lungs made pain shimmer through his body. Any movement brought the pain crashing down on him.

Yet the pain seemed distant. Without moving, without touching his wounds, he knew drugs anesthesized his mind and body, putting distance between his consciousness and the pain. He did not want to test that distance by shifting his body or by moving a hand. Every heartbeat, every breath gave him reason to remain motionless.

But he risked sight. Opening his eyes brought down a hammer strike of pain and he arched back against the agony and more agony came from his arm, his back and his head. For a time, pain held him. Willing himself slack, he waited as the pain receded, then opened one eye to a slit.

Faint gray light. Above him, he saw a progression of rectangles, starting somewhere behind him and continuing past overhead. A black wall cut off the progression. Faint glows of gray light defined the rounded corners of the rectangles.

Air hissed above him. With infinitely slow deliberation, he considered his perceptions.

A jet. He was in a jet.

Summoning up his resolve, steeling himself for the pain, Lyons turned his head. Throbbing boomed against the interior of his skull. Fire seared his eyes. But he completed the turn of his head and looked to the other side of the small compartment.

A gray rectangle was set against the gray background. Lines of light showed where the top of the vertical partition met the curve of the aircraft's fuselage.

Lyons listened and heard nothing but the engine vibration and the hissing of the air-conditioning vents.

He tried to sit up, the pain coming an instant after his chest and arms pressed against the restraints. The straps held his chest, his arms and hands, his waist, his legs. The strap immobilizing his jaws fixed his lips in a grimace. He could not even call out.

His eyes closed, his mind somewhere else in the darkness, he wondered about his wounds. If he suffered this much *with* painkillers, how seriously had he been wounded?

But it doesn't mean a thing, he thought. Because I'm dead meat.

They got me.

Hours before—days before—he had lost a one-on-one duel with Colonel Jon Gunther of the International. Lyons had fought with the intent to kill. But Gunther played a different game on that mountainside. Gunther had waited, hidden by forest and the fog of drifting clouds, his shotgun ready.

A squad of Guatemalan counterinsurgency airborne rangers—traitors who had sold their loyalty to the International—pursued Lyons. An ambush had taken the life of Lyon's friend Nate Beck. Lyons had promised to get Nate's wife and children and sister-in-law out of the mountains. Facing helicopter-borne search teams and more ambushes, Lyons had sent the women and children ahead. With their Quichenero features and indigenous clothing, they could travel without notice.

Could Lyons, the *norteamericano* stranger, walk unnoticed through a checkpoint? Light-skinned, blond, blue-eyed, over six feet tall?

Lyons stayed to delay the trackers. He killed their officer, then faked the squad in the wrong direction while slipping down the opposite mountainside. He almost made his escape.

But Gunther knew Lyons. They had fought before, in the mountains of El Quiche, in Honduras, in the mountains of Sonora, and in the neon highrise canyons of Mexico City. Gunther respected the intelligence and daring of the ex-cop now "specializing" in the world's terrorist wars. Lyons had survived alley firefights and desert action in combat against all the enemies of mankind—Iranians, neo-Nazis, Pol Pot mercs, and outlaw bikers—taking victories in wars never-to-be-known to newspapers and hundred-grand-a-year newscasters.

And Gunther knew Lyons would not allow a squad of soldiers to panic him. Therefore, when the soldiers ran west in pursuit of Lyons, Gunther crept east. As Lyons moved silently down the eastern slope, Gunther shadowed him, watching and waiting for his chance.

When he closed the distance, he fired, hitting Lyons again and again with neoprene riot slugs meant to stun and immobilize, not kill. Then, when Lyons pulled a grenade to end his life rather than suffer capture, Gunther kicked the grenade away and used the butt of his shotgun to coax Lyons into unconsciousness.

And now the International had him.

Lyons expected interrogation by every means available to the doctors and technicians who served the transnational corporation of Klaus de la Unomundo-Stiglitz, a.k.a. Miguel de la Unomundo. Drug injections, electroshock, torture. How long could he take it?

What if they captured Marylena and Nate's children and tore away their skin with pliers? How could Lyons stay silent?

Lyons knew he would eventually break. In time—and the doctors of the International would have months—all men broke under torture. Only the intervention of death allowed a prisoner to escape with his secrets. Lyons knew the doctors would not allow him the mercy of death.

How could he cheat the torturers? He could not move. He could not beat out his brains on the padding under him. He could not chew off his tongue to drown in his own blood.

The time would come. They could not restrain him every minute of every day and night.

The time would come when Lyons could somehow throw himself from this life. But not now....

He would wait.

He would have months.

4

In the last hour of night, Blancanales drove through one of the service entrances to Aurora International Airport. They had driven straight from Huehuetenango, stopping only for gasoline, coffee and to call Antonio, an associate who worked in the aircraft hangars.

When Blancanales stopped the car at the sentry post, Antonio gave them a salute from the sentry booth. The paramilitary police manning the gate did not approach the car. One soldier pushed down the crossbar, then turned his back as the car passed behind him.

A sliding door stood open at a hangar and Blancanales paused on the asphalt service lane. The headlight of a motor scooter appeared behind them. Slowing, Antonio pointed to the open hangar, then guided his scooter inside. Blancanales followed him.

The tall, lanky Guatemalan pushed the door closed. He had not shaved and a dark stubble shadowed his face, which seemed unnaturally pale in the harsh mercury-arc lighting. Throwing the heavy latch, Antonio started toward the rented car. Gadgets motioned him back.

"Let's go in the office."

"Sure—who're the other people?"

"Who?" Gadgets put his arm around Antonio's shoulders and turned him around.

After his partner led the Guatemalan away, Blancanales and Xagil helped the women and children out of the back seat. Still half-asleep, rocking the children in their arms, Marylena and Juana looked around them, blinking against the glaring light. They did not believe what they saw.

A private jet, light gleaming from the polished fuselage and wings.

Blancanales hurried the group to the steps. Marylena hesitated to go up the ramp. Xagil cajoled her in Qui'che, making a flying gesture with his free hand. Juana beckoned to her from the jet's doorway. Afraid, Marylena looked to Blancanales. *"No problema,"* Blancanales assured her. *"Es facil. Es gratis."*

Only after he told her the flight would be free did the young mother go up the steps. Inside, Juana and Xagil marveled at the luxury. Marylena only took a seat and nursed her baby girl.

When the pilot saw the *indigenas*, he asked, "Is this authorized?"

"Will be when we get there."

Then Gadgets ran up the steps. Antonio shoved open the hangar door and the jet taxied out. Xagil and the women laughed as the jet lurched over the asphalt, then shrieked as the pilot gave the engines power.

In the air, the Quicheneros stared down at the lights of the city. But Gadgets looked out at the darkness of the highlands. "Hey, Ironman. Where are you, friend? Where are you?" he muttered softly.

5

White light and rock and roll.

The flashing strobe light.

The banging roar of noise, two or three tapes played at once, the amplified cacophony shaking him, making his body twitch and spasm despite the pain from his manacled flesh, making his mind lose all sense of time and place.

He could not focus his thoughts on resistance. He could not will himself elsewhere, to leave his body and the prison cell behind, to float somewhere beyond the light and noise and pain. The sensory attack smashed his self, cut through his consciousness to the animal part of his mind where fear shrieked and clawed at his discipline.

But he could not surrender. He could not scream. The bar taped between his teeth held his mouth open in a grimace. He could not do more than choke on his own noises, the sounds of his pain and rebelling consciousness not heard—impossible in the rock and roll explosion—but felt as the tissues of his throat dried and tore as he grunted out one long scream after another, one scream becoming another. Had moments passed? Hours? Time was measured only in the pain of drawing breath through his burning throat.

But the technicians did not allow him to forget time. Though they did not allow him the luxury of knowing how much time had passed, they came at intervals to accentuate his torture. He did not know when they came or how long they stayed or how long passed between sessions, but the sessions indicated the passing of time.

Unannounced and sudden, they came with buckets, throwing splashes of water over his naked body to wash away the sweat and urine, then applied the cattle prods. Lyons knew he passed out for instants as they jammed the electrodes into his wet skin, his body leaping against the restraints in one spasm, the restraints cutting into his wounds. The one-two of pain and shock defeated him again and again, his throat constricting to scream but his consciousness gone before he could grunt out air.

He woke to the jab of the electric prod, screamed into darkness, woke again, took the jolt, gasped, took more jolts, then finally lay alone again, the strobe light beating at his eyes, the roaring, shrieking, pounding rock and roll continuing.

A snatch of reasoning flashed through Lyons's mind. The technicians came and went quickly because they could not take the noise.

They can't handle it.

Neither can I.

Lyons could not betray his partners. He could not betray Stony Man. He could not tell his interrogators every detail of his recent career, hitting the scum of humanity everywhere on earth.

Because no one came to listen.

No one came to offer him silence and peace in return for information.

Every unending eternity of light and noise and pain smashed down one booming fact. Lyons knew it, Lyons accepted it even as he screamed mindlessly, his screams the only escape for the trapped animal in him.

Ain't seen nothing yet.

This is only prep.

To get me in the mood.

For the bad times.

6

"We've paid out thousands of dollars in front money to sources," Kurtzman told Blancanales. "We put out the word that we wanted information. And all we got was phony stories."

"What stories?"

"All this!" Kurtzman gave his wheelchair a turn. He grabbed a stack of typed sheets, then gave a wheel an opposite spin to turn back to Blancanales. "Paper with words. But nothing there. We checked out the leads. Nothing. Just stories to collect our money."

"Who checked out the information?" Gadgets asked.

"Salaried personel. Men who had no reason to skip an investigation or to make up details. They get paid every week whether they get an assignment or not."

"They know what this assignment was?" Blancanales pointed to the typed words on the top report. "'Journalist taken by guerrillas. North American. Held in mountains.' That could be Lyons. And how's one of your salaried personel going to check that out? We went into those mountains. Unomundo could have a hundred hardsites up there and no one would know."

"Read the follow-up, the second page. Read it and then tell me your travel stories—"

"Spare us the suspense," Gadgets interrupted. "Give the info. Just the facts, man."

"Here it is. That informant never left the city. He wrote the story, had his cousin send it in from Hue-Hue somewhere, then showed up at our man's door to collect on the information. We wouldn't have known, he would've gotten away with it, but he cut his cousin out of two days' bus fare and the cousin came to complain. That's the quality of information the agency's getting out of Guatemala."

Blancanales searched through the pages of typing. "Then there's nothing?"

"Zero. Lyons is gone, disappeared."

7

Silence.

The half darkness of his closed eyes.

The malestrom of drums and voices and guitars had stopped, leaving him in silence.

Not silence. An unwavering electronic tone. What? An ultrasonic drone?

Then he realized the sound came from within his skull. He heard the ringing because of the hours—days—of rock-and-roll noise beating at his ears.

Barely breathing, he lay within the darkness of his closed eyes, the noise from his tortured ears a high-frequency whine in the suddenly quiet cell. He waited for what would happen to him next. More electric shocks? More drugs?

Or the mutilations?

Sensations came. Pain cut through the exhaustion. He felt the restraints pressing his raw flesh. His wounds throbbed. His scream-torn throat ached.

Finally opening his eyes, he saw a single bare light bulb in the ceiling of the cell. The strobe light gleamed unmenacingly in the light, the chrome fixture and crystal bulb reflecting images of the cell.

Lyons looked around the room, his eyes scanning the ceiling and a section of the wall before the movement of his head brought a knifelike pain to his throat. The pain seared for a moment. He held still, his gut knotted against the shock, letting the pain fade. He breathed slowly and coaxed his body to go slack.

Opening his eyes again, he very, very slowly turned his head, feeling a wound in his throat stretch.

He saw blank walls and a door. Vents, speaker housings and what looked like the lens of a camera—all placed where the walls met the ceiling—broke the stark, polished white of his cell.

Polished. The surface looked like white ceramic glaze. Stain-repellent surface. Blood repellent.

When would his interrogation begin?

Lyons tried to inventory his injuries. The pain in his throat. The aching wounds to his back, ribs and arm. His head wounds. The superficial lesions where the restraints had cut him. Even his nakedness hurt, his skin where it pressed against the slimy pads under him becoming one mass of itches.

No doubt about it, he hurt.

But when did the real hurt start?

Time became a sequence of inhalations and exhalations. He let his breathing clock the wait. Other than the ringing in his ears and the rasping of air through his torn throat, he heard nothing.

The polished white walls of the room seemed to echo his breathing. As he lay there, exhausted, aching, pains shooting through him with every inadvertent shifting of his body, he began formalizing his strategy of escape.

He knew his captors wanted him to panic. For that reason, they had allowed his body to metabolize the pain-killing drugs and the sedatives that dulled his mind. Fear required consciousness and imagination. The returning aches and pains would accentuate that fear.

And time. Time without distraction. Time for his pain and imagination and fear to work on his resolve.

They might leave him alone in this white room for days, in silence and white light, to think.

To become afraid.

Of what?

Torture and death.

But he accepted his death. And after the acceptance, how could he be afraid of torture?

Torture would only be increments onward to death. So what if they used the electric prods? Or if they used a "telephone"—one of the electrical generators that allowed the operator to vary the charges shot through the prisoner. If they hit with an overjolt, he might get lucky and his heart would stop. And so what if they cut him?

Mutilation only horrified the prisoner who expected to survive. He had heard the stories, seen the horror in fact, talked with survivors. But if it happened, he would accept it. Mutilation would not break him. Mutilate a corpse, the corpse said nothing. Lyons knew he had died back on that mountainside in the Cuchumatanes of Guatemala. Nate had died to give his family and his friend time. He knew what had to be done and he did it. Now Lyons got the chance to prove himself.

Yet he could not confront the coming interrogation without strategy. He had to delay them until he could escape or die. And the only way to delay would be to talk.

What did he know they would want to know? What did they already know? What could he assume they knew and assume they could cross-check?

The Stony Man operation had been penetrated the year before. Bolan lost people and the operation lost its invisibility. If Bolan's enemies knew and the Soviets knew, why not the International? The main man himself, Bolan, assumed Stony Man had been compromised. Lyons had to assume the International had sources for information and that they would use that information to check his answers.

Therefore, Lyons would tell them everything they wanted to know—as long as time had made the information dated. As long as the information did not endanger his friends. Why not? He only knew about Able Team. And everyone in the government seemed to know Able Team's business; after all, hadn't they been set up for slaughter in Mexico by an agent of their own government? Soon everyone at Stony Man would know he had disappeared. They would cover their operations, shift their agents and contacts to safety. But that would take time.

Stretch out the stories. Give them details that mean nothing. Keep the names of the living, give them the life stories of the dead.

Make time. With time, they would believe he had broken. With time they would begin to treat him like a prisoner. Not a trapped wolverine.

When they gave him the liberty of a prisoner—
the freedom to move his arms and legs, to walk, to
pace a cell, to watch his jailers, to hear their voices,
to study their routines—then he had a chance to
escape.

Escape to freedom.

Or death.

8

On the video monitor, Colonel Jon Gunther saw a bloody and bruised man of thirty-plus years of age, of excellent physical condition, who had obviously—judging by the scars—faced dangerous and potentially lethal circumstances many times in his career.

The naked blond man lay on a white medical table. Nylon restraint straps pinioned his arms, legs and torso. Blood shone at the restraint points. To disorient and fatigue the prisoner, technicians had applied mild electric shocks. The resulting body spasms had caused the restraints to cut the prisoner.

But the abrasions would heal.

Adjusting the transmitter monitor, he heard background noises of breathing and mumbling. In the cell, Carl Lyons talked softly to himself, the words coming unformed and guttural to Gunther. He listened as he watched his prisoner. Lyons lay very still, probably looking around at the absolutely escape-proof cell, listening to the building around him and thinking of his predicament, his fear and panic building by the second.

Gunther touched the video zoom, and went close up on the stitches on Lyons's throat.

No bleeding. The sutures had held despite the thrashing around.

Returning the lens setting to normal, Gunther watched and thought, contemplating his prisoner.

The capture had been exceedingly difficult. Only through his exacting preparations and knowledge of Lyons's character had Gunther succeeded in taking the American alive. The sacrifice of the soldiers had been costly, yet expedient. How else to trick Lyons into believing he could escape? Otherwise, he would have taken a defensible position and fought to the death—as had his friend. The use of the soft, nonlethal shotgun slugs had been absolutely required. How else could he have stunned Lyons into semiconsciousness? The fact that the slugs hit with the impact of bullets had saved Gunther's life. Lyons had come within an instant of killing both of them with a suicide grenade.

But now came the greatest challenge: to create from Carl Lyons a weapon to serve the International.

In Mexico, when Gunther had been the prisoner of Carl Lyons, Lyons had asked hundreds of questions about Gunther's role in the International—his rank, responsibilities, his motivations, the rewards. The questions about the rewards had alerted Gunther to an opportunity. Gunther told Lyons of wages paid in Krugerrands, the one-ounce gold coins of South Africa. Then he had turned the questions on his interrogator. Gunther had asked him what the United States government paid Lyons for his high-risk missions with Able Team.

Though Lyons would not answer, Gunther pursued the subject. He ridiculed the policies of

congressional approval that limited the options of
the Able Team strike squad. He talked of the wealth
of the bureaucrats and elected representatives who
created the problems Able Team countered, then
contrasted their privileged life with the harsh life led
by Lyons: for the politics of others, he faced death
or dismemberment and received only a government salary as pay. And what of the future? Did
Lyons have access to government secrets to guide
his investments? Did he enjoy the same opportun-
ities of a congressman? To earn a six-figure, tax-
sheltered income and to invest that income in defense industries that would multiply his capital in a
few years?

Gunther finally ended his questions with an offer: one thousand dollars a week, paid in gold, if
Lyons would serve the International.

And Lyons accepted the offer.

However, other events had disrupted the recruit-
ment. Gunther had also bribed Juan Coral, a drug-
gang gunman cooperating with Able Team in an
effort to attack the International. Juan Coral
helped Gunther to escape from Able Team, but
only for the purpose of interrogating him. Coral
then returned Gunther to Able Team. In the few
minutes before the climactic destruction of the
Mexico City offices of the International, Gunther
had not had the opportunity to test or even question Lyons.

Had Lyons actually sold his loyalty? Or had the
acceptance of the bribe been only a ploy?

In fact, Lyons had done what had been possible
in the situation. But there had not been the oppor-

tunity to prove his loyalty to Gunther with an absolute test.

Gunther had no illusions. If a man sold his loyalty, his loyalty became a commodity to be marketed again and again. But no one paid more than the International.

And this time, Gunther had more than money to offer Lyons. He would offer Lyons his life. He would offer him freedom from a cell, an end to torture and all the comforts of service to Miguel de la Unomundo.

Lyons's mutterings continued. Gunther turned the volume up slightly. He could not make out any distinct words. Switching off the background-suppressant circuits, he listened to Lyons's heartbeat: slow, steady. Calm.

No fear. Or the control of fear. What sort of man had Gunther captured? Shot and wounded, flown to an absolutely secure cell and subjected to abuse for seventy-two hours straight, then given time to think about his dreadful future—and no fear? No panic?

The next few days would change that. Perhaps Lyons thought the worst had already passed. Gunther keyed the intercom.

"Doctor, begin the interrogation. As we discussed."

"Yes, sir. I am assembling my staff at the moment."

Lyons would know fear soon. No man could not fear what Lyons would soon experience. The pain would be the anvil and the hammer with which Gunther would reform the character of Carl Lyons, antiterrorist specialist. Gunther would smash him

until his sanity shattered. And then he would re-
mold Lyons to serve the purposes of the
International.

No longer would Lyons fight terrorists. In his
new role, Lyons would become the most lethal of
those he had once considered only silhouettes to be
shot down.

He would be an assassin.

9

"Hello, Mr. Lyons. I am Dr. John. I will be working with you in the next few months."

Trying to speak, Lyons heard only a rasp get past the plastic rod barring his jaws. Pain shot through his throat as he raised his head to see Dr. John and two technicians. They all wore white coats. Behind the doctor, the technicians—two white men with bland features and close-cut hair—pushed a rubber-wheeled cart into the cell.

Dr. John leaned over Lyons. The doctor smiled with perfect white teeth. He wore his hair short but parted and styled to the side. His barber had cut his sideburns perfectly. Smile lines radiated from the corners of his pale blue eyes. He had a sportsman's tan.

His blue eyes focused on Lyons's injuries. Smiling, he slowly walked around the table, glancing at the wounds and bruises and bleeding sores. The technicians went through the motions of a familiar routine, positioning the cart, uncoiling electrical lines, taking out bottles of solution.

One of the technicians took a spray bottle and went to each of Lyons's injuries, applying a few sprays of an alcohol solution to the scabs. Though the solution burned, Lyons did not allow himself to flinch.

"That is to prevent infections," the doctor told him with a smile.

The other technician used a second spray bottle to wet predetermined points on Lyons's body—the insides of his thighs, his belly, his fingers, his scalp.

Though the doctor said nothing, Lyons knew the purpose of the solution was to enhance the skin's electrical conductivity.

Despite the pain in his throat, Lyons tried to speak. No time like now to start cooperating. He grunted and coughed, trying to get words past the plastic rod.

The doctor motioned for him to be silent. "Don't try to say anything, Mr. Lyons. I am not an interrogator. I have no tape recorder. That is not my responsibility at all. I only prepare you for the questioning."

Stretching out coil cords, the technicians clamped alligator-jaw clips to Lyons's body. One of the technicians fastened a short strap next to Lyons's head and passed it over his forehead. Lyons could not even move his head.

The technicians took positions at Lyons's head and feet, staying more than an arm's distance away. They looked bored but attentive, performing their duties as trained.

Standing at the machine, the doctor spoke in his pleasant voice. "Throughout all of this, Mr. Lyons, all your time with me, you must remember that this is nothing. This machine leaves the subject virtually unmarked, though in some cases it produces a certain amount of damage to the nerves. However, it also produces effects equaled only by mechanical devices. Though the other devices have very marked and immediate psychological impact, mechanical devices cannot be employed for unlimited periods. This generator can be used, with relative safety, indefinitely.

"My duty is only to introduce you to the process of interrogation—"

The doctor touched a button.

Lyons felt his body explode in a flash of yellow light, the pain too intense to understand, rivers of pain flowing from his crotch to the top of his head, his body thrashing and twitching as he fell through a brilliant yellow universe of pain.

Then it stopped. Smiling, Dr. John looked down into Lyons's face.

"Remember, we will have all the time in the world."

10

On the horizon, the lights of the Triangulo stood against the gray night of the Guatemalan capital. Gadgets sat low in the taxi's seat. The knit cap and scarf he wore concealed his hair and skin. Beside him on the seat, the receiver hissed. Intermittent noises came as the minitransmitter sent the noises of banging sheet metal, barking dogs, music and voices.

Gadgets waited on an avenue in Zone 5. Though only a few minutes from the Spanish architecture and formal gardens of the capital's old plaza, this avenue had no colonial charm. Nor did the street within sight of the ultramodern high rises of the commercial center feature the sleek lines and flash of the twentieth century.

Wind swept dust from the dirt street. Headlights from a passing car illuminated the swirling dust, then the car continued on, its taillights blurred. Dogs wandered from the doorway of a cantina. A woman appeared and stood silhouetted against the dim red light of the interior. Fat, wearing a negligee and panties, she tottered on glistening black spike heels. Light shone through the bubble of her beehived hair. She searched the street for action, then turned and stepped back into the crimson glow. A record came on, blasting out lyrics and electronic rhythm.

Listening, Gadgets struggled to understand the song's Spanish over the noise of the receiver on the seat next to him and the wind banging the corrugated roofs of the shacks along the avenue. Then for a moment, the wind died. He heard only the electronic hiss of the receiver, some background traffic noise and the song.

Donna Summer sang about Sunset Boulevard, and Gadgets realized he was listening to English. Inside the cantina, the fat woman reappeared, dancing with herself to the music, the red light shimmering on the synthetic of her negligee, her breasts swinging independent of her body.

"Oh, too much...." Gadgets put his hand up to block his sight of the image. He kept his eyes straight ahead on the street, watching the line of shacks and plank-wood gates in front of him.

The lights of a jetliner cut across the gray night sky. A few hours before, Gadgets and Blancanales had flown in. Sources had reported a kidnapping gang holding an unidentified North American. The gang had worked both sides of terrorism, kidnapping and ransoming corporate managers for the Ejercitio Guerrilla de Los Pauves and making teachers and union leaders "disappear" for President Lucas Garcia's Judicial Police. In the past two years, the army had eliminated both the EGP and President Lucas Garcia. The unemployed gang needed money so they had kidnapped a *norteamericano*.

Apparently, they had taken the North American about the same time Lyons had disappeared.

After reading the report, Blancanales had made long-distance calls until he succeeded in negotiating a deal, in which a police detective would receive $10,000 for his information and assistance and $25,000 if they succeeded in rescuing their partner. Blancanales and Schwarz flew to Guatemala City and met the detective, who explained that his daughter needed very expensive heart surgery in San Antonio, Texas. Air fare and doctor bills would be many thousands of United States dollars.

Detective Brillas did not care if two Americans denied due process of law to a gang of Guatemalan criminals.

Now, Gadgets waited and listened to Donna Summer, while Blancanales and Detective Brillas reconned the gang's house. Blancanales had placed a minimike on the window of the house, and through the pane of glass, the mike transmitted sounds and voices from within.

But by counting the voices and the sounds of movements in the room, Gadgets estimated they faced no less than three men in the room. He had no way of knowing the numbers of gangsters in other rooms or those who remained silent.

Headlights outlined two silhouettes. As the car passed, the forms of Blancanales and Brillas appeared from the darkness. They walked casually to the taxi and took seats in back.

"See anything?" Gadgets asked.

"A very pretty girl who is very lonely," Detective Brillas answered, nodding toward the dancing prostitute. "Perhaps you would like to meet her."

Gadgets made a face of terror and pulled his wool cap down over his eyes. "Anything but that."

So what goes on inside?"

"I counted three voices. Some movement. Four, counting a new guy. Some dude in a black leather jacket went in while you were checking the other street. See any way in other than the front door?"

"Dogs, both sides. No way from the other street, either."

"Heard the dogs. Too bad we didn't bring knockout biscuits."

"Through the front door? Hard and fast?"

"Ironman-style...."

Blancanales turned to the Guatemalan. "Detective Brillas, we'll be kicking down the front door. There's a chance we can just take the North American away from them without a fight. But if not—"

"It is very, very dangerous," the detective interrupted. "Anything could be in the house."

"Wizard, you saw someone go in there? He go in by the front door?"

"Knocked and walked. That door does open."

"Then there's no booby traps on it. Maybe weapons inside, but once we're inside, we've got them."

"Spoken like the Man of Steel himself." Gadgets commented. "Then, on the other hand, look who's got who now."

"Let's go. Detective Brillas, watch us. The moment we go through that door, drive the taxi up to the house. When we come out, we'll need to go straight into the car. Have the doors open and the motor running."

As he unholstered his silenced Beretta 93-R, Gadgets turned to the Guatemalan. "Remember,

Detective. The money's in our pockets. You don't get us out of here, you don't get paid."

Detective Brillas smiled. *"Claro.* Of course. I understand perfectly."

"Then let's move," Gadgets said as he shoved the Beretta under his belt and swung open the door. In the street, he checked his pockets.

In his left-hand coat pocket, he had two Italian MU-50G controlled-effect grenades. The tiny grenades, designed for the close-quarter combat of antiterrorist actions, held a forty-six-gram charge of TNT to propel 1,400 steel balls. The reduced charge of explosive limited the one-hundred percent kill diameter to ten yards. Perfect to clear a room.

In his right-hand coat pocket, he had one "white light" flash-shock stun grenade. This grenade had no shrapnel at all and relied on its ability to produce a deafening blinding explosion of overwhelming noise and white flash guaranteed to stun and disorient anyone in a confined area.

Gadgets pat-checked the extra magazines of subsonic 9 mm rounds in his pants pockets, then gave Blancanales the nod. As they walked toward the gang's shack, Gadgets scanned the windows and doors of the other houses on the street. No one. The dancing girl had even closed the door of her cantina.

They made no effort to walk silently. Broken glass and stones crunched beneath their feet. They maintained a steady, unhurried pace to the door.

Suddenly throwing himself sideways, Blancanales hit the door with his shoulder, breaking wood

and crashing metal. He cut to the right. Gadgets
followed two steps behind and cut to the left.

Several men sat on chairs in a room watching a
television. Two middle-aged Hispanic men had the
scarred faces of career criminals, their jowls hanging and their pot bellies ballooning beneath their
dirty T-shirts. A third man, in a leather jacket and
tight jeans, wore his hair in an Afro.

The two Able Team vets saw no *norteamericano*.

But they did see three pistols appear. Gadgets did
not break stride as he rushed past the men, spraying 3-shot bursts of 9 mm point-blank into the faces
of the men. Pistols fell from the hands of dead men
to clatter on the floor. Behind him, Gadgets heard
Blancanales fire a coup-de-grace burst, but he did
not look back as he hit the next door.

The door flew open, and Gadgets stumbled
through a bedroom and crashed into a dresser.
Bottles of cologne, hand mirrors and framed photos smashed. Someone shrieked and Gadgets saw
forms move in a bed. One form reached for a holstered pistol hanging on a chair. Gadgets sprayed
two bursts and hit the arm, snapping bones while
other slugs knocked hunks of plaster from the wall.
He dropped out the spent magazine and jammed in
another as he rushed the bed.

A man cried and pleaded, his voice shaking with
fear. Gadgets jerked back the tangled sheets and a
naked girl shrieked and crawled from the bed.

Blancanales flicked on a light. In the bed, they
saw a blond, fair-skinned young man. He had the
tan of a beach boy. Muscles stood out on his
shoulders. One arm flopped as he held out his

hands and begged, *"Por favor, no. Yo tengo mucho, mucho dinero, no matame—"*

"Oh, shit," Gadgets said. Who are you?"

The wounded man switched to English. "You're Americans? Why the hell did you shoot me?"

"We're here to rescue you, you dumb shit. Why'd you have a pistol? That's why you got shot." Gadgets kept his Beretta pointed toward the two, pointing the muzzle first at the blond man, then at the dark teenage girl cowering against the wall.

"Rescue me? How did he ever find out where I am? Why didn't he just pay the money? That bastard! That devious old bastard, he sends you hit men and takes the chance that I'm going to get killed? Why didn't he pay? I'm his only son and look at me! You shot me, you shot me!"

Blancanales shook his head. "Time to go, partner."

"Shit!" Gadgets cursed again. He backed out of the room, his pistol pointed at the bleeding man.

The gunmen sprawled where they had died, pistols showing, pools of blood forming on the floor beneath the corpses. The dim light of the television played on the men's dead eyes.

Blancanales and Gadgets rushed through the smashed door and stepped into the waiting taxi. They slammed the doors and Detective Brillas floored the accelerator. Dust clouded behind the taxi as the tires spun in the dirt, then the detective threw the car into a hard right-hand drift. In seconds, the taxi merged into the traffic of a boulevard and left Zone 5 behind. Gadgets leaned forward and gripped the Guatemalan detective's shoulder. "Sorry, Brillas. You get your base fee, but no bonus."

"But that was the right address, yes? And that was the gang, yes? And did they not have a *norteamericano*?"

"Yeah, they did…but they can keep him."

11

They allowed Lyons to move within a cell.

Now he had the privileges of standing, walking, sitting or lying down.

As a staring video lens monitored his movements, Lyons had complete freedom, with a few exceptions.

On the bed, he could not turn his back to the bare light set in the high ceiling. If he did, a remote-controlled siren and electrodes studding the bed shocked him awake with a simultaneous high-decibel shriek and a jolt of electricity. He had to keep his face to the light. He had not slept in the days or weeks since they put him in the cell.

For hours at a time, in between interrogation sessions, he paced his cell, exercising his legs on the spongy padding of the floor. Sometimes he played "bounce," running at the wall and bouncing off the plastic padding, throwing himself into the opposite wall and bouncing again, back and forth until his body ran with sweat.

Not a great game, but the only game in town.

There was another limitation to his freedom: he had no hope of escape from the cell, not even the illusion of opportunity. The cell had no window. Air entered through a line of vents no more than a finger wide along the floor. An exit vent along the ceiling pulled out his expelled air. The door operated electrically, with no edges to grab, only soft resilient plastic.

Neither was there any hope of escape by death. The cell had no sharp edges or hard surfaces. His prison uniform, some sort of clothlike plastic, could not be torn into a hanging rope and no fixture or window allowed a knot to secure a noose. A toilet hole in one corner of the cell did not have the diameter to allow suicide.

So he amused himself by playing bounce or staring at the walls. With his mind twisted by the drugs and exhaustion, the white walls became floor-to-ceiling televisions, complete with stereo sound and transcontinental linkups with his friends elsewhere in the world. He talked and laughed, and when the technicians came for him, he went.

Sometimes it was the chair, sometimes the table. He saw a variety of technicians and machines. Drugs were injected and jolts of electricity applied.

Electric torture. Low power meant pain and stiff muscles from his body jerking around in the restraints. High power meant a minute or two of sweet, dreamless sleep.

Drugs meant his perspective changed, his memories changed. But the pain remained the same.

"I'm cooperating!" he screamed, repeating the words again and again until his voice trailed off into obscenities and stream-of-consciousness details about life as a cop in Los Angeles. The faceless voice of the interrogator calmly led him back to the question.

"But I asked you about Lebanon. Who was your liaison in Beirut?" The voice of the interrogator came from behind blinding lights. Lyons never saw who questioned him.

"A raghead! A whole family of ragheads! Making money off the agency...raghead Arabs..."

"Names!"

All ragheads...Mohammed Abdulla that, Mohammed Abbalula this—"

Current surged through him, jerking his head back, his teeth snapping, every tendon in his body going taut for an instant as a painlike flame consumed his body.

Darkness. A time of peace. The horizon-to-horizon belly of the Caribbean, his head on the thighs of Flor as the sun...

Water splashed him, trickled over his bound legs. The water tasted of salt, and salt enhanced conductivity. His hands hurt from clawing the arms of the chairs. His spasms had opened the scabs on his wrist where the restraints secured his arm in session after session.

"Names!"

"Like I told you, contact Jon Gunther. He'll tell you about me. He's with the International. You're with the International, right?"

"I ask the questions."

"Then ask Gunther about me! We had a deal and then he screwed it up and it's not like I can contact him! You know what happens if I make a phone call and my people are surveilling me, just to check up on me and they tape that call? I get the toaster treatment, just like now. Now I'm getting it, anyway, and if you call Gunther he can question me and I'll talk to him and you can save on all the electricity, understand? This is unnecessary! You're frying me for nothing!''

"Answer the questions."

"I answer the questions but I can't give you names I never had and my head's so scrambled I couldn't remember even if I ever did know the names. You can't keep doing this shit to me and expect me to give you any information of value. My head's going funny farms—you understand?''

"I ask the questions. I want the names of your contacts in Beirut. What was the name of Lieutenant Powell's friend?''

"Powell? Powell who? Was he—''

Nerves leaped out of Lyons's flesh in networks of incandescent pain, the fine lines of fire spreading in radiating shatter-webs across the backs of his eyes and his body turning, falling backward somehow, his consciousness recording the fact that his legs kicked and jerked and his arms spasmed against the restraints even as darkness took him.....

He woke panting, gasping for air, water flowing down his body again. No, not water, his own sweat.

"Tell me about Powell, Mr. Lyons."

"Powell was a Marine lieutenant. Stayed on after the pullout, working some kind of liaison deal for the agency, working with the Shia Amal against the Shia crazies, I could never figure out what he was talking about—they all talked the same shit as far I could understand—''

"Names, Mr. Lyons."

"Don't hit that button! Don't. Let me think for a second. Why don't you let me sleep for a while? I've got to know the names, I heard them, but my mind's all screwed up, my mind's all..."

12

In an office bright with afternoon sunlight, Jon Gunther discussed the progress of Carl Lyons with one of the doctors supervising his case.

"How does he respond to the electric shock?" Gunther asked.

The doctor thumbed the pages of Lyons's folder. "Oh, as they all do."

"Why have you not progressed to intermediate voltage?"

Startled by the question, the doctor hesitated an instant before answering. "Eventually, I will, but—"

"Levels equal to his discipline might produce a change."

"Levels equal—you mean, extreme voltages?"

"Extreme voltage does not necessarily involve injury."

"All my experience and study indicates otherwise." The doctor straightened in his chair. He touched his necktie and ran his hand down the lapels of his white lab coat.

"Then it may be unavoidable. To a point."

Tapping the typed brief on the first page of Lyons's file, the doctor stated, "That contradicts your instructions."

"Synthesis...a synthesis, that is what we want."

"How do you mean, sir?"

"It must be believable, that we believe him."

"Then you are instructing me to increase the settings to the point of injury?"

Gunther did not answer for a moment. He considered his problem. Lyons must think that his interrogators believed his statements of loyalty. However, no interrogator would believe an unbroken prisoner. The prisoner must be broken, smashed, his character destroyed, all previous beliefs and loyalties reduced to zero. Lyons knew this.

But Gunther could not destroy Lyons. To execute the mission Gunther had planned, Lyons must retain his intelligence and daring.

But he must also do exactly as instructed.

In a sense, the mission required a new Lyons, a synthesized Lyons—one whose character was a combination of daredevil and automaton.

This required that the interrogators achieve a precise effect: stress Lyons until his character became malleable, and to the point that Lyons believed he appeared broken.

Perhaps the sham required injury. Sleep deprivation and mild electric shocks did not physically destroy a man. If Gunther relented at this point and accepted Lyons as a comrade of the International, Lyons might suspect the validity of his membership. But if the interrogators increased the severity of the shocks—perhaps to the point of superficial burns but short of actual nerve damage—and Lyons faked a collapse of resistance, then he might believe that they thought his surrender genuine.

Nodding, Gunther returned his attention to the interrogator. The balding, middle-aged doctor had reviewed Lyons's file while his superior considered the options. He made notes as Gunther issued his instructions.

"Increase the severity of the shocks until the applications produce burns. Consult your records and attempt to predetermine a threshold of nerve damage and then never approach that point. Closely monitor his physical condition. Do not allow his health to collapse. Use drugs to induce dreamless sleep, to allow his body to rest, but create the illusion of no time having passed while he slept, so as to heighten perception of fatigue and to throw off his body cycles. I want him to be in pain, disoriented and psychologically ready for a breakdown.

"Then push a session to the limit...."

13

Lyons floated, his eyes staring at the slick white plastic ceiling, his fatigue and the drugs breaking his vision into swirling white points, the points swirling around him like snow as if he was floating in a warm, white void.

The pain of his body meant nothing to him. He existed in lights and pain, he existed in darkness and the absence of pain. Consciousness did not flow from one state to another. The Lyons of each state did not exist for the Lyons of the other.

Memory failed to distinguish single incidents when all incidents appeared identical. He did not know whether they questioned him during the day or night. He did not know the time, or what day, or month he was in. He could not measure time by his sleeps because he did not sleep.

When they came for him, he went. The lights remained the same. The voices questioning him sounded the same. If he had remained conscious of the sessions, he would have been aware of an escalating intensity to the electric shock. Now, in addition to the button electrodes strapped to him, they used cattle prods and alligator clips. Fists came out of the lights to emphasize certain questions. But darkness always took him.

Unconsciousness gave him rest and release. They could revive him from that darkness, but they could not follow him.

And in those few seconds of unconsciousness when he approached the threshold of death, his mind cleared and he became a man again. He saw his friends, he relived scenes of his life. Then the technicians revived him and the questioning started again.

He no longer feared. During hs interrogation, he had gone through phases of fear. In Guatemala, before his capture, he wanted to die because he feared torture. In the first phase after capture, he feared the failure of his sham because the torture would continue if they did not believe him. Then came a period when he realized they did not care about his proclaimed loyalty to the International. This period became very bad because he could not understand what to say to stop the torture. Finally he transcended fear.

When they came for him, he went. When they strapped the electrodes to his body, he did not resist. When he answered the questions, he did not fear the interrogator's response. If the interrogator believed him or if the answer corresponded to their information, he did not get punished. If he hesitated to answer, or if the answer did not match a previous answer, or if the interrogator thought he lied, he got pain. He had received so much pain that he no longer feared it. He took it as it came. And sometimes, when the interrogator exceeded Lyons's physiological limits, Lyons received a moment of darkness far, far away from the pain.

Lyons existed from moment to moment, concentrating on his breathing. They fed him, they showered him, technicians cut his hair and fingers and toenails, doctors examined him daily. Deep in his mind, past the exhaustion and drug fog and pain, he knew they would not kill him by accident. For a while, he had hoped they would shoot too much amperage through him during a session, but he had abandoned that hope. Now he knew they would only kill him when they finally tired of questioning him.

When they came for him, he did not hear the door open, he did not hear their soft-soled shoes on the padded floor. Faces appeared over him and hands took him and pulled him upright. When they shoved him from the cell, he lurched into the corridor, walking like an automaton.

But Lyons had not quite surrendered. Somewhere in his animal mind, he wanted to survive. His eyes always searched for the way out. He listened. Shuffling to the interrogation room, he scanned the corridor.

He saw closed doors, a door open to reveal a windowless office, a heavy door with a lever handle and a lock. A view hole at face height provided for a security check of anyone on the other side. No sign identified the door as leading to an office or a cell. He had never seen that door open.

Hands behind him directed him into the interrogation room. Blinking against the searing lights, he walked toward the chair. But today, a table waited in the center of the room. He went to the table and touched its gleaming surface.

Stainless steel.

"Strip him."

The technicians pulled off his drawstring pants, jerked his shirt over his head.

"Strap him down in an X."

Again, the technicians obeyed the instructions. They lifted him onto the cold table and buckled restraints over him. Lyons did not resist. No point. Then the technicians squirted conductive water over him. He waited for them to strap on the electrodes.

A doctor—not as tall or muscled as the technicians, wearing glasses, his fine-fingered hands holding a syringe—stepped up to Lyons. Holding the syringe off to the side, he checked Lyons's pulse with his free hand.

During the delay, Lyons studied the syringe. A disposable plastic syringe, it held a clear fluid. A drop of the fluid ran down the needle, light sparkling through the drop.

The doctor pinched Lyons's arm to raise a vein, and Lyons felt the scabs from previous injections crack. Sliding the needle into the vein, the doctor slowly drove down the plunger.

Lyons's heart hammered. His body went taut, his eyes wide. The scene of the room around him seemed to shift. Pulling out the needle, the doctor looked down into his face, then gripped his wrist again to take his pulse. Lyons felt his heart thrashing in his chest.

The doctor stepped back and the interrogator spoke from behind the lights: "There is a phone number and access code for direct telephone communication with your command center. We have that phone number and access code. Answer this question. What is the verbal code to arrange a meeting?''

Lyons did not answer immediately. He saw a technician step forward with a prod, the perspective of his silhouette and the speed of his step strange. His words stopped the prod in midair. "There is no code. It's my voice."

A hand appeared from behind the lights and made one quick gesture to the technician.

The prod went to Lyons's genitals. The shock and pain arched him upward against the restraints. The technician held the prod steady even when Lyons jerked and flopped like a fish.

His consciousness did not leave him. Pain beyond anything before arced through his body. He felt his muscles and tendons spasming.

Against his genitals, the prod seemed to become a sun radiating incandescent flames of pain. But still Lyons did not pass out. Somehow distant from the scene, he heard himself screaming, he felt his body beating against the stainless steel tables, every flop and spasm jerking him against the restraints, then smashing him back down into the stainless steel. His breath came in pants, his screams dying to the squeaks of a small animal.

He smelled burning flesh. Still he did not pass out.

The technician stepped back. Suddenly still, Lyons went slack, his body trying to curl into fetal position, but the restraints stopped him. He lay staring at the patterns of light on the ceiling, his breath coming in quick panting sobs, the pain in his crotch like fire.

"The code for a meeting."

"...voice...they know my voice...we're friends...no code..."

"That is a lie—"

Lyons thrashed, expecting the prod to come next.

"—We know a Guatemalan called with the code and summoned your associates. The Guatemalan called and they came immediately. What was that code?"

"It wasn't...a code," Lyons gasped. "It was a message that—"

The prod hit him in the crotch again, the pain making his body jerk and thrash. Somehow, the pain doubled and Lyons realized the second technician had jammed another prod into his stomach. As the prod slid up Lyons's body, he smell burned meat as he screamed and tried to run away from the pain approaching his face but the restraints held his body and his consciousness held him.

He screamed without end and the interrogator screamed down into his face. For once the interrogator had a face and Lyons saw his lips moving as he demanded, "What is the code?"

The second prod burned up Lyons's neck. He thrashed his head back and forth trying to shake the point of arcing fire from his body and then it touched his face and the technician leaned his weight on it to pin Lyons's head motionless.

Skin sizzled and burned and Lyons screamed and shrieked and pleaded in a voice no longer human, without words, only screams and shrieks and sucked-down breath and begging as his mouth filled with the taste of burning meat.

And the point of fire moved toward his eye as the interrogator leaned down and shouted, "The code! The code! The code!"

Lyons screamed. "The Ironman needs you! The Ironman needs you! That will..."

And the points of arc-flame-pain went away.

"...that will get them...they'll come..."

The interrogator nodded. "Good. You could have saved yourself a very unpleasant experience if you had only answered immediately."

His pulse hammering, the afterimages of a whole new world of pain still flashing on his body like neon, Lyons gasped down breath after breath and thought; Hope you make that call, Mr. Interrogator. Hope you give them an address. Hope you're waiting there for your experience. Because they'll know it's a phony.

14

Kurtzman took the call. A tape machine automatically recorded the voice as other circuits traced the signal back to the point of origin and recorded the number.

"The Ironman needs his partners. He'll be at—" The voice gave an address in Miami.

"That's—" Kurtzman repeated the street number and name as if writing the information down. "Okay, I got that. But who are you?"

The line went dead. Kurtzman checked the readouts. He had the area code and phone number. Then he rerecorded the message from the master tape to several cassettes. One cassette would go for voice-graph analysis cross-checking. Others would go to Federal agencies for their analysis and cross-checking against voices on file. One would go to Blancanales and Scwharz for their comment.

"It stinks," Gadgets commented an hour later. "Ain't him and ain't anybody we know."

"A pay phone," Blancanales said considering the message. "And the word 'Ironman.' Whoever called doesn't necessarily have Lyons. But they know he's missing. Have there been any visits from congressional oversight committees? Has Brog-

nola put out the word to the Feds about Lyons?
Who would know he has disappeared?''

"Only the people at Stony Man," Kurtzman
answered.

"Then it could be whoever got him." Blancanales glanced at Gadgets. "What do you think?"

"Could be who this, could be who that. Don't
mean shit. We go, it's an ambush—no doubt about
it.''

Blancanales feigned shock. "I hadn't thought of
that. That means you want to avoid this
appointment?''

"Means I want to load and lock before I make
my appearance. Any chance of Phoenix backup?"

"Those guys are off at the moment. But Encizo's with family in Miami—'

"Perfect!" Blancanales said. "Give him a call."

"Better than perfect," Gadgets laughed. "That
Cuban's almost as vicious as Lyons. This could be
a good time."

FOUR HOURS LATER, as the sun sank into the
swamps, the two men of Able Team met with Encizo and his friends in a suburban parking lot.
Teenagers skateboarded past the group of men as
they talked strategy. Blancanales sat on the fender
of a rented car studying a street map as his partner
briefed the others.

"It's a setup," Gadgets told the others. "I am
one hundred and ten percent positive. You know
this place? What's the scam? Why's there only one
street going in?"

"Private neighborhood," Encizo answered. He pointed out the location on the map Blancanales held. "A security community—"

"Thought so," Gadgets said as he nodded.

"Armed guard at the gate. Patrols. Don't know how we could even get in to back you up unless we put on delivery uniforms or drove pool cleaners' trucks, that sort of thing. And no one cleans pools at night."

"Yeah, but people party," Gadgets countered. He snapped open a briefcase and took out a stack of folded cards and passed them out to the several men. "I brought invitations...."

Encizo glanced at the embossed card. "Convenient...but no address."

"Got it covered." Gadgets took a movable type hand stamp from his briefcase. "When you get me a name and address, you get your invitation personalized."

"Convenient. We'll make calls. Someone has to know someone who's living there."

Within an hour, the three cars of men sped north on the interstate. They wore casual dinner clothes and cologne. Several carried bouquets of flowers, others gift-wrapped bottles. All the cars had Able Team hand-radios. When they pulled off the interstate, two cars parked, allowing the first group of Cubans to go first. Five minutes later, Encizo and the others followed. Finally, Gadgets and Blancanales drove their rented car to the guard post of the private community.

The white-haired guard leaned down to look at them. "Quit a shindig in there tonight, eh?"

"Lo siento, señor," Blancanales answered. *"No hablo ingles."*

The guard looked at Gadgets. "Can you translate for your friend?"

"Ich kann nicht Englisch sprechen."

"Tower of Babel, that's what this country's coming to," the guard muttered, waving them on.

They entered a neighborhood of mansions. Million-dollar homes lined the side of the street fronting on a waterway. The other side of the street had what looked like a private park screening the exclusive development from the frontage road. Decorative lights spotlit architectural showcases. Entryways looked like movie sets. Some homes had the obligatory Rolls-Royces and Mercedes. Others had the masts of the family yacht showing above the rooflines.

"What do you say, Pol?" Gadgets scanned the homes. "Think we can afford this on government pay?"

"Depends on the government. Not U.S. government."

"Maybe we could go private again. Kick ass for cash."

"I like my job."

"Benefits are okay. Travel's great. But the people we meet are real scumballs. If I couldn't kill them, I'd quit."

"And when you've killed them all, you're out of a job."

"There it is. But it won't happen. Scumballs breed, man. They breed faster than maggots. Always be more scumballs. More scumballs than bullets."

"Pay attention, Wizard. We're working."

"I can work and talk, too. I ain't the average government worker."

"Quiet!"

They heard a popping. Gadgets flipped aside the coat covering his Beretta 93-R. He reached under the seat and pulled out a bag. Inside the bag, they had two loaded mini-Uzis, several magazines taped end-to-end and a plastic bag full of MU-50G grenades.

"Ready!"

"Up ahead," Blancanales said as he put his mini-Uzi in his lap. He let the car coast onward.

With the car windows open and the warm, humid air blowing over them, Gadgets and Blancanales listened. They heard only the tires of the car on the asphalt. Then came the sounds of music: the notes of electric guitars, a drumbeat, a voice.

Pops took their attention. A series of staccato cracks broke the music. The the drumbeat continued; the singer did not stop. More pops came.

Blancanales glanced at Gadgets. "Firecrackers..."

"A party?" Gadgets pointed to a driveway.

Encizo stood at the curb, a wide circular driveway behind him crowded with parked cars. Blancanales braked to a slow stop. The professional freedom fighter leaned into Gadgets's window:

"Compañeros, here is the party."

"A real party?" Gadgets asked.

"There is a band, there are girls, even firecrackers. It is a party." Encizo lowered his voice. "And down there is your address."

Leaning across the seat, Blancanales spoke quietly to Encizo. "What have you seen?"

"Nada. No cars, no people. Lights in the house, but I see nothing moving inside."

"Your people ready to go?" Gadgets asked. "Or are they making the scene, drinking that booze?"

"They drink a little. But it makes them brave. Okay?"

Blancanales shook his head. "Get them out of there. We don't want brave men, we want back up."

"Sí, comandante." With a salute, Encizo walked up the driveway to the house.

"Cuban jivesters," Gadgets laughed.

Looking past the house to the other address, Blancanales scanned the street. He saw lights in the windows, but no cars in the driveway. No cars parked on the street. Across from the house, in the landscaped green strip, he saw rolling lawn and shadowed clusters of trees, highlighted by points of decorative lights.

"Give me odds," Blancanales told Gadgets. "There are lookouts in the dark over there." He nodded toward the trees.

"Forget the odds. Call for a pizza."

"What?"

"Yeah, a pizza. Have it delivered to that house over there. They waste the delivery boy, we know it's an ambush."

Blancanales shook his head at the suggestion. "I've got Encizo's Cubans drinking and my partner is volunteering innocent teenagers to take point into a suspect ambush. I thought we were professionals."

"Innocent teenagers? Hey—" Gadgets pointed to his own chest "—I was an innocent teenager, and I had everyone—my squad leader, my lieutenant, my captain, my colonel, my President of the United States—I had everyone volunteering me into ambushes. Let some local kid get his dose of bad times—"

"Wizard, that was Vietnam. That was a war. And you were in the Army. There is no comparison."

"Dig this, I enlisted to learn electronics. Fight communists, sure. They're bad for radio reception. But—"

"Shut up! Cover up the weapons—there's a car coming up behind us...."

A private patrol car sped past them. The patrol car braked in front of the house where Lyons supposedly waited for them. The emergency lights flashed. Hands on pistols, two uniformed security guards ran to the house.

"Maybe Encizo called," Gadgets wondered out loud.

Their hand-radio buzzed. Encizo spoke to them. *"Mes amigos,* there is nothing in that house."

"How do you know?" Blancanales demanded.

"One of my men, he did not want to wait. So he went and he looked. The house is empty."

"Get him out of there. There's two private cops going in with pistols."

"Oh, he knows. He tripped the alarms after he got out."

"So there's no one in there?" Gadgets asked.

"No one."

"So, my friends," Encizo told them through the radio, "this was for nothing."

"Not for nothing. See you in a moment." Blancanales pocketed the radio and motioned to his partner. "Come on, we're invited to a party."

15

Lyons woke to a room with a view. He turned in the bed—it had a pillow, sheets and a cover—to stare out at the expanse of lawn and flowers. Blooming flowers lined a walkway cutting across wide lawn. A stand of trees walled off the distance.

A wind stirred the trees. Birds cut the blue of the sky. The line of flowers moved with the wind.

Turning back to the room, he saw a telephone on the bedside table and a drinking glass filled with water. He reached out to touch the glass and pain flamed through his shoulder. He moved more slowly. Flicking the glass with a fingernail, he heard it ring like a bell. Glass. Breakable glass. Glass that could slash. They trusted him with glass.

He tried the switch of the bedlamp. The light came on. Picking up the telephone, he heard a dial tone. He scanned the room and saw an armchair, a doorway to a private bathroom, a writing table and a door to the outside. He did not see a monitor lens.

Flinging aside the cover, Lyons lowered his feet to the carpeted floor. He had aches and pains everywhere. His torso had a long, wide Mercurochrome-painted burn starting from his navel and going up his chest. He felt scabs on his neck and the side of his face.

He pulled open the underwear he wore and looked down at himself. He saw more scabs and Mercurochrome, but no serious damage.

Steadying himself, he tried standing. Tight muscles and pain made him stagger, but he forced himself to walk to the bathroom. In the mirror, he saw that the prod-burn went to within an inch of his right eye.

Scabs ringed his wrists and ankles where the restraints had cut away his skin. His back had gone purple and yellow from bruises caused by thrashing on the steel table. Bruises, burns, cuts, scrapes.

"Did they do a number on you," Lyons said to himself in the mirror, his voice raspy and cracking.

Going to the center of the room, Lyons stretched, carefully exercising his abused body, twisting his torso, touching his toes. The light stretching produced a series of new pains. Then he went throught slow, very slow isometrics.

A knock on the door interrupted him. He waited for someone to enter. No one came in. They knocked again.

"Come in," Lyons finally said in his hoarse voice.

The door swung open. Filling the doorway, Jon Gunther stood without moving for a moment, then stepped inside. He smiled and extended his hand. "My friend Lyons, how are you? Think you'll recover from the stupidity of those doctors?"

"Yeah, I guess. But what was the point? I told them everything they wanted to know. I cooperated. But I got the routine, anyway—"

"I know, I know. I found out when I returned. I must apologize. When I captured you, I described you as a prisoner. I should have—"

"So it *was* you on that mountain."

"Could I have sent anyone else to pursue you?" Gunther sat in the armchair. "You would have killed them. As it was, it cost me a few dead Guatemalans to trick you, to play your game. And you came very close to killing me, also. But that is all in the past."

"But you shot me. How did I live through that?"

"Plastic bullets! Don't you, as an ex-police officer, have experience with those?"

"Not on the receiving end."

"There was no other way. And though the past few weeks were completely unnecessary, consider the treatment your debriefing. No one can question your conversion to the International."

"I kept telling them—"

"I know, I know. Of course, it will be months before you receive a security clearance, but consider today your first day with the International. You'll stay in this room while you recover. And we will continue your debriefing, though in a manner far less demeaning and abusive.

Gunther stood from the chair. Shaking Lyons's hand again, he started out. "I will be gone again for a few days. Travel, you understand. But now that I have clarified your status, I am sure you will find your membership far more agreeable. Adios."

As he closed the door behind him, Gunther pointed to the bedside telephone. "You can call room service for anything you want."

Lyons watched Gunther leave, then walked over to the phone and picked up the receiver.

"Room service?" Lyons said to himself, rubbing the scabs on his throat. He felt a new scar and lump, perhaps from the fight on the mountain.

"Yes, sir," a voice said over the phone.

"What time is it?"

"Four thirty-one in the afternoon."

"Too early to order dinner?"

"No, sir. I have instructions that you are to receive whatever you want, twenty-four hours a day."

"Great. I want dinner. What is there?"

"Whatever you would like, sir."

Lyons decided to test the kitchen. "Assorted sushi—including sea anemone and salmon eggs— lobster teriyaki, brown rice, a liter of saki, a color television with a video deck and some cassettes of the latest movies."

"Yes, sir. The brown rice is unusual—it may take a few minutes. Colonel Gunther assigned a physical therapist to you. Perhaps you'd like," the voice continued, "her to give you a massage before dinner."

"Oh, yeah? Well, might be better than television. Send the saki right now."

"Yes, sir."

Minutes later, Lyons answered another knock. The therapist stood six feet in her nurse's shoes. The white uniform did not conceal her figure or her sensuous walk as she pushed a cart into the room. She wore her blond hair cut fashionably short and only a touch of blue mascara around her eyes.

"Hi, specialist. I'm Cheryl. And it's my job to take care of you." She glanced at the burns on

Lyons's chest, neck and face. "What happened to you? You look like you got attacked by a toaster."

"You haven't seen the worst of it."

"Oh, I think I will," she replied with a grin.

16

Heavy breathing and gasps filled the interior of the windowless cubicle. Gunther and the technician exchanged glances. The balding, middle-aged technician folded his hands over his beer gut and rolled his eyes.

"He's having his fun," the technician joked.

"Cut out the woman. I want to hear only his breath and pulse rate."

"Done."

Hitting switches, the technician electronically removed the voices and enhanced Lyons's breathing and pulse rate. They heard his measured breathing and low, steady heartbeat.

"An athlete," Gunther commented as he switched off the monitor.

The technician laughed. "So is she."

The tape recorder continued turning, the needles of the audio meters continued jumping. The faint squeaking of the tape reels cut the sudden silence.

"Let's allow our guest some privacy," Gunther said, smiling. "Though I don't understand the electronics involved, I would say that what we heard certainly proves that the device operates as expected."

"There's more than microelectronics involved," the technician said as he pointed to a rack of gray consoles. "We employ two computers, with a third as backup. The dual-channel format allows for computer redefinition of the signals. If we had to automatically adjust the levels on a single channel while he talked to pick up the other voices and sounds, the quality would drop off radically. As it is, with one channel carrying his voice only, the computer can monitor and modify the incoming signal of the second channel. The computer strips the background noise from the first channel. Then the second computer eliminates the sounds present on the first channel from the second channel, which leaves the other voices and sounds. It's the audio equivalent of computer-enhanced photography combined with computer-generated video special effects. Done instantly."

Gunther only nodded as he leafed through a casebook, noting the observations of the technicians monitoring the receivers. "And the directional signal?"

"He hasn't been off the grounds," the technician said with a shrug. "How can we properly test it? I'd like a field test in an urban area. Complete with radio interference and building shadows. The worst possible environment. Otherwise, overconfidence could lead to disappointment. And the loss of your specialist."

One page took Gunther's attention. He glanced at the series of photos, then read the text. "There's no chance of an accidental triggering of the termination charge?"

"Absolutely none!" The technician pointed to the page. "There is an encoding circuit that absolutely eliminates any possible accident. There are multiple codes and a required sequence. If the charge does not receive the codes in sequence, there will be no detonation."

"Unless someone attempts to remove the device…"

"That's different. But there's even a few safety features incorporated to prevent an accident. We didn't want him cutting himself shaving and taking off his head."

"Then it's absolutely safe until it's absolutely lethal."

"Exactly. Absolutely."

17

The immortal tones of Charlie Parker shot through Gadgets's head, notes starting in one headphone and screaming through to the other. Nodding along, he sketched scenarios of the mystery of Lyons's disappearace, the outlines looking like microchip schematics. In his imagination, he established circumstances and ran Lyons through a maze of confrontations and characters, trying to create a vision of what had happened to his partner.

One long, neon tone lasted too long for a scenario, became a circle of pure light, like Lyons fighting an endless series of skirmishes in a Central American slum.

The strobe on his answering machine flashed, and Gadgets took off the headphones and blinked away the nightmare. Crossing to the machine, he clicked the switch over to monitor.

The voice of Kurtzman, coming metallic and impersonal through the NSA scrambler-encoder, dictated a message onto the tape. Gadgets was in time to catch the words "...that the house next to the one designated as the meeting place had also been entered. But not by burglars. The security people found a—"

"Found a what?" Gadgets broke in.

"Interested?"

"I answered the phone, didn't I?

"Those Cubans didn't have any photo or electronic equipment with them, did they?"

Gadgets laughed. "They had pistols and bottles and maybe some women. It was a serious party."

"Well, the men who set up an observation post in the other house didn't go to party. After the police searched the house and left, neighbors reported that men with equipment cases left the other house."

"So?"

"Doesn't that fire your interest?"

"Forget the interest. I don't have to wonder. I know what went on."

"And that is?"

"They called, we went to check them out and they checked us out. We got faked by a fake. Could've been worse. Maybe they took my picture. So what?"

"I think they wanted to know if you would show up if they called this number and gave Lyons's name," Kurtzman said.

"Now they know. Or they could've just figured to have a shoot-out some other time."

"Maybe," Kurtzman replied.

"And maybe we'll find out for sure."

"When?"

"When they come shooting. Now leave me alone—I'm working."

"Working on finding your partner?"

"Wasn't my idea for him to take a vacation in Central America. Let him find himself."

"Cold, Gadgets. Glad I don't work with you."

"Yeah, me too. Wish I didn't work with myself. Talk to you some other time."

Hanging up, he returned to his headphones. He put his mind to the mystery again.

What had happened to that jerk?

Who got him? Where did they have him? What was going on? How could they get him back?

He thought of Lyons chained up in some jungle shithole and wished he had put his friend on the wrong plane: a direct flight to Disneyland.

Safe, hygenic, plastic Disneyland.

18

Waking with Cheryl's arms around him, Lyons looked out on the mooonlit grounds of his prison. Ornamental lights sparkled along the walkways and in the darkness of the trees. He did not see any other buildings.

Shadows passed on the walkway. Lyons caught only the jagged silhouette of two men walking side by side. Security? Doctors out for a midnight stroll, between torture sessions? The Pol and Wizard infiltrating?

Forget the fantasy. They don't even know if you're alive. And if they did, so what? You don't know where you are.

Scanning the trees that blocked the horizon, he saw no lights that might indicate a town nearby. He had studied the section of night sky visible from his bed, but couldn't make out any star patterns. Even if he had found north, he did not have the skill to determine his position by the stars. But then again, he knew his position.

In prison. Location of prison unknown.

After talking with Gunther, Lyons knew the International held him. All the expensive technicians and the blond women, the estate, the jet—these were the assets of Trans-Americas, S.A., the trans-

national corporate front for Miguel de la Unomundo. Like the International Battalion in Sonora
and the Trans-Americas tower in Mexico city. Assets. Tools to be used.

Need a facility for meetings and computer ter-
minals? Build a skyscraper in the capital of the
Western Hemisphere. Got a prisoner to entertain?
Send him a "therapist." Got a reporter writing
disturbing articles? Send a death squad.

Cost meant nothing. Unomundo had billions.

And now Unomundo had him.

But why had the interrogation stopped?
Throughout the questioning, he had always told
them of his loyalty. They hadn't believed it. If he'd
been questioning an opponent, he wouldn't have
believed it. Too easy.

Then again, one point worked in his favor. Since
the hit on Mexico City, Able Team had worked
outside the hemisphere. Aside from two in-and-out
hits—one in Nicaragua, one north of Mexico City,
both against Soviet-sponsored opponents—Able
Team had worked away. Beirut, the Bekka Valley,
Syria. An extended mission into Asia.

There had been no confrontations with International forces. Maybe Gunther thought Lyons had
directed the Team away from International operations. Or maybe Gunther thought the work in the
Middle East and Asia kept Lyons from contacting
the International.

Or maybe nothing. Gunther could be running a
game on Lyons. Trick him into giving information. Maybe this night of good times would play a
part. Torture, then presto-changeo! The luxury
suite, with Sushi, saki and sucki.

Presto-changeo worked both ways. He could get another encounter session with the hand-held toaster tomorrow. Or two minutes from now. With Cheryl doing the toasting. But then again, things could be worse, as the Wizard often said.

I could be back in the white room, waiting for the questions.

19

Thousands of flashing lights shimmered in patterns creating words and scenes and geometric shapes. The crowd screamed. The personalities shrieked and flashed white smiles and posed in motion for the cameras.

Video technology made the scene more than real. All the screen personalities had perfect tans—some real, some cosmetic. And they all wore the latest expensive fashions—courtesy of the sponsors. The crowd always laughed or cheered at the appropriate moment, cued by stage technicians with signs.

Marylena turned away from the television. Cradling her baby in her arms, she walked to the window and stared out at the night gray of Baltimore. The night had no stars, no moon, only the vague gray of overcast and pollution. On the next block, a few trees stood against the gray, the lights of an apartment house making the trees glow green. Every leaf glistened. She stared at the trees as she rocked her baby in her arms, the voices and recorded music of the prime-time entertainment only noise behind her.

"What's wrong?" Blancanales asked Xagil in Spanish. "I know she can't understand it, but a television's a good way to learn English. And to see how the people in this country live. Maybe she'll like it if I find a Spanish language—"

The boy answered in his own Quiche-accented Spanish. "We are not Castilian. We don't want to hear Spanish."

"Is there something wrong with the television? Is there a cultural problem? Is it against your customs?"

"The television means nothing. She does not want to be here."

"She'll like it soon. America has everything—"

"No!" Xagil spoke sharply and both Juana and Marylena turned and watched as he spoke. The inane program continued behind his voice. "This is a bad place. No mountains, no forests, no rivers, no winds, no stars, no fields. All the people are different and do not talk with each other. The men on the street touch Marylena, they have no respect and I have no machete or rifle. There is no work for Marylena or my mother and no work for me and no people we know."

Taking the remote control, Blancanales punched the off button. As a starlet turned in close-up, her perfect features, perfect makeup and perfect hair superimposed on a brilliant blue background, her lips moving to form a word, the screen went black, and only a glowing point remained. Then the screen faded to gray. "But it's not safe for you in Guatemala. You know what could happen to you if you go back."

Juana spat out a Quiche obscenity. She had understood the *norteamericano*'s words. Speaking quickly to Xagil, she gestured at Blancanales. She argued with her son, then motioned for him to tell Blancanales.

"My mother says this is a prison. If we go back and we die, that is the way of life. If we stay here, we will certainly die, our souls will wander forever in this prison. We will go back to our mountains."

Shaking his head, Blancanales started to explain. "There is a problem. My partner—"

Juana interrupted. "We walk! But we go."

"No, when it's safe to go back, we'll take you. That is not the problem. The problem is this. The men who attacked you took Mr. Stone. He is their prisoner. Or perhaps he is dead. We hope not. They will question him. He will not tell them what they want to know, no matter what they do to him. He will die before he talks. But if you go back, and they take you, that will give them power over him. If they take you, then Mr. Stone would talk. Do you understand? When we know he is free—or dead—then you can go back. Is that good enough?"

Xagil explained to his mother and Marylena. They nodded.

"We will wait. And my mother says I will go with you to help find Mr. Stone. He was a good friend to us."

Blancanales nodded. "He was a good friend to me, too."

20

Throughout the morning, Lyons ran and walked the perimeter of the sprawling estate. The soft lawns made a perfect jogging track. And jogging around the fences gave him the opportunity to check and recheck every detail of the estate and the perimeter security systems.

No one accompanied him. Cheryl had told him he had the freedom of the estate. He could go anywhere but out.

For the first time, he saw his prison from the outside. The brick buildings stood four stories. He looked for a windowless section, but saw only conventional buildings. The main buildings all had windows. Perhaps the cells and interrogation rooms—which had no windows—had been built into the basements.

A long driveway led from the guarded gate and then divided, one branch curving to the entry and a parking lot. The second branch continued past the buildings to a modern concrete parking structure. He saw the phosphorescent orange sock of a helipad flying on the roof of the parking garage.

The buildings occupied the center of an estate hundreds of acres in area. Lawns circled the buildings, the expanse of grass extending to the fences.

The lawns created a perfect field of surveillance from the windows. No one could cross the expanse unobserved. The lawns also created a perfect field of fire.

Electronics and soldiers guarded the perimeter. Lyons recognized two different sensor systems on the wrought-iron bars—pressure sensors and infrared beams created invisible lines a few inches inside the fence.

On both sides of the perimeter, walkways parelleled the fence. A band of close-cropped lawn separated the walkways from the fence. Lyons guessed those bands of lawn hid more pressure sensors. Anyone approaching the fence, from the inside or outside of the estate, would trigger the buried sensors to alert the security force. Video monitors stood on poles.

Lyons saw the security force everywhere. Men in sports clothes walked near the fences. Others manned the guard positions. All the guards already knew him. They waved to him as he ran past. One introduced himself and said, "Welcome to the International. We're already bigger than some countries, and in a few years, I bet the corporation will own a few."

"Yeah, that's why I'm here. I want to be on the winning side."

"You made the right choice." Then the guard leaned close and spoke quietly. "And don't think this is some phony Nazi outfit. The Third Reich never had decent leadership. They had the spirit and will, but the crazies dragged them down. You already know Colonel Gunther. When you meet some of the other leaders, you'll know what I'm telling you is straight. You wait. You'll know. You'll know that what Mr. Unomundo says will happen."

The other guards had not talked to Lyons, but Lyons recognized the high morale and discipline. All the guards wore crisply pressed slacks and sports coats. Unlike the doctors and technicians in the buildings, all the guards maintained excellent physical condition. No one slouched. He saw no overweight men. When he ran past a guard station, he saw no one reading newspapers or magazines. The men stayed alert, watching the private roads approaching the estate and glancing at video monitors.

Though he saw no weapons, he knew the coats covered pistols and that the guard houses would have rifles and perhaps antitank rockets.

Beyond the fence, he saw trees, snatches of rolling fields, and another fence. He saw the wide asphalt surface of a landing strip. Once he caught sight through the inner fence and the screen of trees of a car patrolling the outer perimeter.

No one could crash this installation. Maybe an airborne assault. But Lyons knew they would have antiaircraft weapons concealed somewhere.

Lyons ran and walked for hours, thinking, searching for a way out—and a way in. If he managed to break out, he wanted to come back and inflict payback.

Like shoving that high-voltage cattle prod up the ass of Dr. John and cooking him slow.

Cheryl interrupted his running. Today she wore a white miniskirt that cut across her thighs and white tights. She had the top three buttons of her crisp white shirt open, revealing the curves of her breasts. Lyons remembered the feeling of her body the night before, her thighs locked around his head. He said nothing. He walked up to her and held her.

Impulsively, she took a lick of the sweat on his face. "Hey, specialist. Tasting good again. They want you inside for some questions—easy! Don't worry."

"You never got the treatment. Easy for you to tell me not to worry."

"If they doubted you, you think you'd be romancing one of the nurses?" She kissed his throat, touched his ear with her tongue, took another lick of the sweat coursing down his beard-stubbled face. "I mean, when I gave you the treatment last night, when you were jumping and screaming, you liked it—am I right?"

Lyons thought of his hands knotted in her hair as her lips clenched around him and his orgasm threw him back against the bed.

"Come on," she said, leading him away, hand in hand. Like teenage lovers, they walked to the door of the hospital wing. She took him around a corner, but stopped short of the offices and pushed open a door.

A supplies closet. Lyons glanced around and saw stacks of linens and paper towels. He looked back. Cheryl stepped out of her white tights, leaving the tights loose around one ankle. Lyons pulled the bow knot of his drawstring and stepped up against her as his sweat pants fell.

Standing against a rack of plastic-wrapped pillows, they grunted and heaved. Cheryl tried to put her leg over Lyons's shoulder and kicked down bundles of foam bed pads. Laughing, she braced her foot against the shelf and ground her groin against the wall of pillows.

"You're a good time yourself."

"How many times we make it last night?"

"I don't know. How many times for real? And how many times in my dream?"

"You dreamed about me?"

"This is all a dream."

Must've been a long time since you were with a woman."

"Yeah, that's a fact."

A minute later, Lyons was staggering down the corridor, sweat soaking his workout clothes. Heels clicking on the linoleum, Cheryl walked beside him, grinning at him.

"In there," she said as she pointed to an office. "And remember, tonight it's aqua therapy."

"Too much."

She laughed and left him at the doorway. Pausing first to gather his wits, Lyons opened the office door.

Lights!

Someone laughed. "It's not what you think, Mr. Lyons. We need the lights for the camera. This is not a hostile interrogation."

Lyons walked in. Dr. John sat at the desk. A technician stood behind a video camera. "Then what is it?"

"I will ask you questions, and we will tape you as you respond. Won't hurt a bit. Please sit there."

A chair had been placed directly in front of the camera, and sitting, Lyons found himself looking directly into the lens. He could see his distorted face in the element.

"I want you to look at the power light on the front of the camera, directly above the lens. My assistant will also attach some other devices. Please keep your eyes on that point of red light."

The technician wrappped blood-pressure cuffs around both of Lyons's arms. Miniature bands went around two of his fingers. Another strap pressed a disc of metal into his right palm.

For the next hour, the doctor went down a list of questions. He and the other interrogators had asked the questions many times before, and Lyons had always answered the questions more or less factually.

Lyons kept repeating to himself that the Soviets, the Congress, and many of the Capital journalists already had the Stony Man details. Why not use the old information to buy his way into the International? Why get the toaster treatment for what they could read in the newspaper?

The doctor made no comments as he listened to the answers. Lyons knew that the camera recorded the dilations of his irises and that the other devices monitored his pulse, blood pressure and sweat.

Wired for truth. But Lyons cheated. From time to time, he glanced around the room. Looking at one of the lights, then to the doctor, he got an idea.

The technician motioned to the doctor. The doctor politely reminded Lyons, "Please keep your eyes on the light.

"I'm going cross-eyed."

"We're almost done...."

As he answered the questions, Lyons calculated distances and angles. Planned his moves. Had to be smooth. Didn't want them to think he did it deliberately.

"And that's the last question. Thank you, Mr. Lyons. You may go now."

The doctor wrote notes on the sheets of questions. The technician switched off the lights. Lyons stretched out in the chair, his body only contacting at the edge of the seat and the top of the back, and yawned.

He hooked the tip of a shoe under the thin, folding leg of a light stand.

And flipped it.

Lyons watched the light fall, willing it to target.

Then the impossible happened. The power cord stretched tight, causing the light to pivot as it fell. Lyons had hoped to have simply the light *stand* fall on Dr. John.

Bent over his notes, the doctor did not sense the falling light until the incandescent hot glass bulb touched the top of his head with a loud hiss of cooking hair and flesh, then the light smashed.

The doctor screamed and grabbed the formed-aluminum reflector that crowned him.

His hands sizzled on the hot reflector.

Screaming, crying, blood and hot glass everywhere, the light stand clattering, the doctor fell backward in his chair, smoke curling from the top of his head.

"Oh gee, doctor! I'm really sorry!"

Lyons struggled to keep back his laughter as he went to help the screaming man.

"Does it hurt?"

21

"The light hits his head and he screams and he reaches up and grabs it!" Laughing, Lyons slapped the water for emphasis. "The room smelled like a barbecue!"

Naked with Lyons in the hydro-massage pool, Cheryl laughed. Lyons reached for his beer on the edge, turning sideways in the churning, steaming whirlpool. Across from him, Cheryl slipped lower in the water and entwined her legs with his, then twisted to throw Lyons under the water.

Splashing and sputtering, Lyons turned to grab her, but Cheryl laughed and writhed until she released him.

"You do a different style of judo," Lyons commented.

"Love judo." Cheryl splashed across the pool. She drank the last of her beer. Her lithe, full-breasted body steaming, she left the pool and crossed the room to the massage table. Drying her hands, she opened up a smoking kit.

"Sinsemillian with opium?" she called out. "Or with hash? I've got coca paste, too, but that's really heavy. I save that for weekends. Unless you want to try some."

"I don't do dope."

"Better than beer."

"When I want to get stoned, I booze it."

"And get a hangover. Haven't you ever tried smoking your good times instead of drinking?"

"Smoke that shit, I go crazy. When I was a cop, we'd smoke sometimes and go roust deadbeats. Tried some when I worked with the Team, but that was different. Go crazy with auto-weapons and high explosive and you got pieces of people everywhere. Out of control. No *bueno*. Had to quit it."

Cheryl came back with a hand-rolled cigarette and a lighter. "I want to see you go crazy. You're not doing anything now. Nothing but me."

"Crazy. I mean, I go crazy. It would be rough."

"I like it rough. And if you get rough, I can stop you."

"All right..." Lyons reached for the cigarette.

"Don't touch it—you'll soak it. I'll get you a towel."

"And get me another beer, could you?"

"We've killed the six-pack. I'll call for an orderly to bring in some more."

"Hey! Don't do that! I don't want the colonel knowing about what's going on."

Cheryl laughed. Lyons knew why. The colonel already knew about Lyons and Cheryl because the colonel had assigned Cheryl to Lyons. But instead of saying that, Cheryl assured Lyons, "It's okay. I know her. She won't say anything to anyone. In fact, I bet she'll want some, too."

As she talked on the intercom, Lyons scripted out his stoned and drunk routine. After all the drugs the interrogators put into him, he had no interest in adding marijuana, opium, hashish or cocaine to his blood. And he wished Cheryl wouldn't either.

But Lyons would play the role of a doper. If the International let their people party with dope, then he'd play the role.

When Cheryl returned, she exhaled smoke as she placed the cigarette between Lyons's lips. He faked a drag, inhaling through his lips, then pulling a mouthful of smoke and blowing the smoke at Cheryl.

"Like it?" she asked, pulling down another hit.

"Feel it already. Give me another."

"Don't touch it. I'll hold it."

Lyons faked another drag. He pulled smoke into his throat and exhaled through his nose. Cheryl alternated with Lyons, Lyons making a show of his smoking. They smoked the cigarette down to a butt. Then they heard keys at the outside door.

"That'll be Luisa."

A plump, dark-haired young woman wheeled a cart into the therapy room. The cart carried two six-packs of beer and a bottle of vodka. Luisa spoke with a slight Spanish accent. "Hi, lovers. So this is why you scheduled this place. What're you smoking?"

"Flowers and opium."

"Dreamy. Am I invited?"

"Sure," Lyons answered, the word coming very slow and strange. He realized that he had actually inhaled the drugs. Oh, well. Once won't make me a junkie. "Come on in."

"I will!"

"Yeah, okay," Cheryl agreed. "I have another smoke rolled and waiting."

Lyons watched Luisa strip and wondered if Gunther had assigned her to him, also. As the clothes came off, Lyons became more interested. The young Hispanic had womanly thighs, and round, uplifted breasts, and a slim waist. She kicked her underwear away and brought a six-pack to the whirlpool.

"So you're the specialist," Luisa teased, pulling the tab on a beer can and passing it to him. She popped open another for Cheryl. "What's so special about you?"

"I shoot straight," Lyons said, pointing an index finger at the young woman's forehead.

"What's so special about that? Lots of people shoot straight. A little girl won at the Olympics, shooting straight three hundred times in a row."

Taking a long gulp of beer, he gave the question serious consideration. They expected him to brag. One naked man with two naked women in a Jacuzzi. Stoned and drunk. So brag. Gunther probably had microphones implanted in Luisa's beautiful breasts. No, one microphone and one infrared skin temperature stress scanner.

"She did it at the Olympics. I paradrop into Nicaragua with eighty pounds of weapons and ammunition. I walk all night through Commie territory; I carry that eighty pounds of weapons up into the mountains. I set up my machine gun and I wait until the sun comes up and when it does, I shoot straight for about an hour and when I'm done shooting, not much is shooting back. And so I walk out. But now I've got only about thirty pounds to carry because all that other weight is in the bodies of about three hundred Commies, holding them down to the earth. I did the same sort of thing in the Amazon, except it wasn't so simple. And in Syria and in Mexico, and that's why I'm special. Because if you give me a target, it's like voodoo. Nobody knows how, but it gets done, that's why I'm special. What do you think, am I so special?''

"Wow, you've been around."

Lyons studied her left nipple. Erect. Standing at rigid attention. Like an inch-long black microphone. Either she had been carefully trained to respond to her subject's answers or she liked war stories. A dirty war groupie. Tell her more. Make this a storytelling party.

"You like war stories?"

"Better than reading paperback romances," Luisa giggled, her round breasts jiggling on the steaming surface of the churning whirlpool.

Cheryl put her arm over his shoulders. Possessively? She passed the glowing cigarette across to Luisa. "Don't get it wet or I'll make you roll the next one. Tell me a story, lover."

Okay, I'll tell you a story, one that Gunther already heard, Lyons thought. "I was in on the rocketing of the Iranian embassy in Syria. Dig it. We dropped ninety-six 240-millimeter artillery rockets, guidance assisted, on those ragheads. High explosive, white phosphorous and gas. Did the number on them. Saw the satellite photos later. The one that missed came down on the North Korean and South Yemeni embassies. Neat, huh? Does that make me special?''

"But the newspapers said it was the Syrians shooting at someone else. That it was an accident."

"What do you expect them to say? That some Americans strolled into their country and took a righteous shit on the Iranian embassy? You figure it. The fighting was in the Lebanese mountains. How could the Syrians point their rockets the wrong way? Oh, yeah, maybe the Muslim Brotherhood did it. They're fighting the Syrian army, trying to take over the country so that they can make an Islamic republic just like Iran. And the Iranians are helping them. So the Muslim Brotherhood launches a rocket attack on their friends the Iranians. Sure, that makes sense."

"Maybe it was the Israelis," Cheryl suggested.

"Believe what you want. You want stories or what? I've done a lot of things, and none of them are boring."

He saw Cheryl and Luisa exchange a glance. Luisa took drag after drag on the cigarette. She finally passed the butt back to Cheryl. "Sounds fascinating...do anything in El Salvador?"

"That where you're from?"

Luisa giggled. "Not me. I'm from Brooklyn."

"I've done things in Brooklyn."

"Haven't done me," she laughed.

"Give me your address."

"About one arm's reach in front of you."

"More like one foot," Lyons said as he touched her with his right foot. Luisa took the foot and closed her thighs around it.

Throwing her empty beer can to clatter on the tiles, she said, "This may be a party yet."

22

Night and screams. Night without stars or hope of day. The night of a cell, a pit, a closed place stinking of filth and fear.

He screamed again and the darkness took his voice, his breath rushing from his body and his lungs seizing, his body twisting and heaving as he panicked, his hands clawing at the darkness but gaining only pain.

Then breathing, sucking down breath, the breath searing his throat, what he breathed a vile miasma stinking of disease and decay. He coughed and choked and vomited the filth from his lungs and twisted in the darkness, trying to breathe, trying to escape the miasma, trying to escape the darkness.

But his movement got the attention of his captors. Kicks slammed into his body. He doubled, gasping filth, laughter coming from above him as the kicks continued. Kicks to his head made the darkness flash with moments of light. He tried to shield his head with his arms and hands jerked his arms behind him.

A boot came down on his back as hands levered his arms back. He felt other hands wrapping twine—no, wire around and around his wrists. Someone laughed as the wire went tight. He felt

pliers wrenching the wire tighter until his hands
became throbbing masses of pain.

They jerked his arms higher and higher, lifting
his body off the slimy stone. His wrists went over a
cold hook and he heard a pulley squeaking as his
arms went up, his arms twisting in his shoulder
sockets, the pain arcing through his arms and
shoulders and torso.

Then came the unseen electrical fire, the pain
sudden and impossible, his body jerking and
spasming as the voltage seared its way through him.
He jerked and spun in the darkness.

A screaming, shrieking man wailed unintelligi-
bly somewhere far away. Spinning in the darkness
with his own pain, the fire attacking him everywhere, laughter and voices in the distance. Then he
realized he screamed and he awoke.

Blinking at the darkness, his throat tight, his
arms aching from a workout with weights, his body
running with sweat, Blancanales felt fear for Lyons
that he had never felt even for himself in all the
years of fighting and horror.

It all came quick in a fight, the noise and blood
and pain were things that ended. But in his dream
the pain and suffering could be escaped—Lyons
could not escape because they had him.

Now, concentrating on slowing his breathing,
trying to stop his own panic, Blancanales thought
of what he had experienced in his nightmare.

Blindfolded in a stinking cell. His hands wired
together, his arms bent back and a hook and rope
jerking his body into the air, his torturers laughing
as they zapped him with electric shocks.

A nightmare.

But in fact, it would be worse.

They had taken Lyons weeks ago. If Lyons had broken, he had already died. If he hadn't, the horror continued, his interrogators moderating the torture only to allow his life—and hope for life—to continue.

But Lyons had no hope unless his partners got him out.

His breathing finally slowing, Blancanales stared out at the stars, wishing his vision could fly through the night like a bird of prey to search the earth for his missing friend.

Lyons, where are you?

And what do you suffer?

23

"So, Mr. Lyons," Colonel Jon Gunther asked. "How does your recuperation progress?"

Lyons laughed. Leaning back in the office chair, he folded his hands behind his head and grinned. "Are you serious? Don't you know how the girls are taking care of me?"

Gunther smiled. "If they want to romance you, that's their business. But—"

"Why didn't you offer me this deal in Mexico? You offered me a thousand dollars in gold a week. You didn't mention the perks! You think the U.S. government treats me like Cheryl and her friends take care of me? Colonel, I would have carried you out of Mexico."

"Good. I'm glad you're happy. But this is not a vacation. I assigned Cheryl because I need you in working condition."

"For what work?" Lyons went serious.

"Work similar to your previous actions, except—"

"I won't kill my friends. I'll recruit them, but even if they won't go for it, I won't hit them."

"That will not be necessary."

"What do you mean?"

"I hope they will eventually join us, but—"

"Then they're still out there? You didn't try to hit them?"

"Why? Do you think they are a threat to us?"

"Not really. But the assholes who tortured me wanted an assembly code. As if they could just call my partners and say, 'Report to this ambush.'"

"No, we don't want you to ambush your friends. We have a target for you and we need your support."

"Who's the target?"

"Does it matter?"

"No, not really. If it's the President, you better have good logistics, because that kind of hit you don't get away from. They chase you to the end of the earth and then into space."

"The assassination of the President? No. He's with us."

"Then who?"

"An enemy to be eliminated. And that's what you will do. I'll take you out to the grounds to show you."

As they walked through the building, Gunther explained. "We will use a long section of the drive leading to the garage as a rehearsal area. The action only requires you to shoot once, but that one shot must be perfect—both in aim and in timing."

"I'll have a mock-up to practice in? A building, a street, or what?"

"Not exactly. The distances will be correct. We will position automobiles to simulate a street. There will be steps to indicate the entry of an apartment house. We will position light posts to exactly duplicate the obstacles on the street. You will not arrive there and find a No Parking sign blocking your line of fire.''

Lyons nodded, silently considering the dilemma the assassination presented. Gunther had no intention of revealing the target. He had said only that the hit would eliminate an enemy of the International.

Who? An investigator or journalist threatening the International's invisibility? An FBI officer too close to proving a case? Maybe a senator or congressman talking too loud and too often about links between the fascist organizations of the Western hemisphere? Or a witness to fascist crime? Or a foreigner, an exile from a nation dominated by the fascist allies of Unomundo?

Who?

Lyons would not know until he saw the face of the target in his rifle sights. Could he do this? Murder an enemy of the International, someone whom he would otherwise defend?

He felt sure Gunther intended to test him with this crime. Lyons had undergone drug and torture interrogation, lie-detector tests, sexual overstimulation—all to confirm his statement that he wanted to join the International, that he wanted the gold, girls and the chance at a rank in the fascist army of Unomundo. Gunther intended to test his allegiance, and trap him in the International. This killing would be different than any killing done with Able Team. This killing would be murder.

Gunther knew it. And Gunther—with every official in the International—would know Lyons had killed the man. Assassination meant murder with special circumstances. Lyons faced execution for proving his loyalty to the International.

But the assassination would be his key to the International.

Did his entry into the International justify killing an innocent man or woman?

If he succeeded in penetrating the fascist organization and somehow getting close to Unomundo, close enough to kill him—would the greater good balance the murder of the unknown target?

And if Lyons did not kill the target, Gunther would only find another marksman to pull the trigger.

The target would be dead whether Lyons killed him or not.

Then again, why not suspend the decision until he learned the identity of his target? He might learn the target's name during the rehearsals. He might guess the identity of the target from the location of the hit. Or he might recognize the target as he sighted his rifle.

Lyons would wait until he knew the identity of the target before he accepted or refused the assignment. Until then, he would go through the motions.

Dodging the morality of the decision? Maybe. Why not? If he refused, Gunther would probably eliminate Lyons. Death. Opposed to the only chance he would ever get to kill Unomundo.

Why not dodge the decision? Wait until the last moment to decide to live and murder or not and die. Wait.

Silent with his thoughts, Lyons followed Gunther from the building and across the grounds to the area between the central cluster of buildings and the recently added parking structure.

There, on a hundred-yard stretch of two-lane asphalt, two of the estate security men measured off distances. Gunther called out to the nearest man, "Have you marked the positions?"

"Yes, sir. We are double-checking now."

"To what tolerance?"

"Plus or minus two inches." The man held up the metal surveyor's tape he held. "To compensate for the curve of the measuring tape."

"That tolerance acceptable to you?" Gunther asked Lyons.

"Depends. Sounds okay. Tell me what goes."

"Take the positions marked on the diagram for two men near the steps," Gunther told the security men.

They waited as the two men went to a place on the walkway marked with chalk. Gunther led Lyons to a chalk mark thirty yards away on the opposite side of the lane. Gunther spoke quietly so that the others could not hear.

"You will be here, in a parked panel truck. A foreign national—the man with his back to us—will confront the subject. He will point a pistol at the subject. He will take money from the subject. Then he will shoot the subject with the pistol.

"You will simultaneously fire one round from your rifle into the forehead of the subject—"

Lyons nodded. "In case the street punk doesn't kill the man with his pistol, my bullet will."

"The subject could conceivably be wearing a bullet-proof vest."

"What caliber pistol? Nine millimeter?"

"Twenty-two."

"No way! That's even worse than nine millimeter. Even if I hit the man in the forehead, a twenty-two won't be a positive kill."

"The slugs you will be firing will be entirely capable of killing with one hit."

"But will they match what the punk's shooting?"

"In velocity, no. But the barrels of the pistol and the rifle will match. And impact and deformation will obliterate any microscopic differences. Investigators will believe a criminal murdered the subject during a common street crime."

"But the punk will know the facts. What if they get him?"

"That will not be your concern."

"You mean, someone else offs the punk?"

"We will have a man in position to attempt an arrest. In the course of the attempted arrest, the criminal will force the officer to defend himself. The criminal will not survive. Does that satisfy your interest?"

Lyons considered the distances and the positions of the two men. "The basic plan's okay. It makes sense to use a punk and then off him. Open-and-shut case. But I don't like using twenty-twos. What will be my weapon?"

"A suppressed Winchester target rifle with a Starlite scope. Will that be adequate?"

"How about prepositioning a homing beacon in his back pants pocket? I'll launch a $555,000 anti-aircraft missile and just blow his ass away. I don't need a Starlite scope! That's Pentagon thinking. For a hundred-foot shot, I can use a rifle with open sights. Work better, too. And I don't want to put a silencer on it. Maybe a length of plastic pipe to hide the muzzle-flash, but if the punk's popping off with his pistol, everyone'll be hearing shots, so they won't know where mine are coming from.

"Look, Colonel, here's how I want to do this hit…"

24

Flames whipped from a devastated nation. Corpses and ruins covered the scorched landscape. Rivers of blood flowed. Mountains of bones extended into the smoke-gray distance. Bombers flew through the rising columns of flame and smoke.

In the center of the death and devastation, a phalanx of black-uniformed warriors threatened the onlooker with rifles flashing with bayonets. The soldiers framed the white-clothed leader, the Savior of the Nations, the Commander of the Armies of the International—Miguel de la Unomundo.

Below the mural, in the richly appointed study, Miguel de la Unomundo sat at his desk, glancing through the report on Carl Lyons, the antiterrorist operative captured by his Director of Security, Colonel Gunther. He read quickly, pausing to re-read some sections and to examine photos.

The colonel waited in a leather-and-walnut armchair two steps from the desk. He watched the wind sway the trees outside the study as his leader reviewed the file. Past the drawn-back velvet draperies, afternoon light bathed the Virginia countryside. The slanting sunlight cast shadows over the walnut-and-gold-leaf paneling of the study and splotched the blood-red carpet.

Turning away from the spring landscape, Colonel Jon Gunther looked at his commander. He saw an enigma. To him, Unomundo seemed simultaneously very young, yet aged. The man had gold-dark hair and fine features, inherited from his Castilian-Guatemalan mother and his German father. Impeccably groomed, his face tanned, his neck perfectly proportioned to his athletic shoulders, he looked like a playboy playing at executive.

But Unomundo had proved himself to be a consummate executive. His father had been a daring officer in the SS, yet had not gained wealth through enterprise. The wealth came from his aristocratic wife, a white Guatemalan debutante fascinated by the scarred young officer's stories of combat against the Soviet armies of the East. Their son had used the family's money to create a transnational corporation now controlling hundreds of billions of dollars.

When Unomundo looked up, Gunther saw the eyes of an aged, cruel, other-than-human creature. Gunther had seen eyes like those impassive interrogators who could watch the reactions of a mother as assistants stripped the skin from her child. Men with eyes like those served the International in El Salvador by raping teenagers, then dismembering the young people alive, the eyes of the killers never looking away from the horror, never lingering on the butchery as would psychopaths, but simply seeing the product of the actions and continuing to create more horror, as ordered.

The old photos of Stalin condemning millions of Russians to unimaginable suffering and slow death in gulags showed a man with eyes like those of

Unomundo, a dictator who could look upon the living nightmare he created without compassion or psychopathic amusement, only seeing his product as he continued to create more hell.

Gunther glanced up at the mural above Unomundo. The man intended to create hell, and from the ashes and bones create his Reich.

"Will this man kill the senator?" Unomundo asked.

"I believe so. He knows it will be the proof of his allegiance to the International. He only asked if he would be the President of the United States."

"He accepts some targets and not others?"

"No. He did not reject the possibility. He did not believe anyone could make that particular kill and escape. He seemed to only be concerned with escaping."

"And how did he react to the plan you presented?"

"With no question as to the target, only to the technicalities. He immediately changed the weapon specifications and revised the scenario for the better. He had absolutely no objections to killing the target, only to the method. He is training now for the assassination."

"Is this man ours now?"

"I cannot answer that with certainty. He professes loyalty. If I consider his actions in Mexico as required for his role, then those actions did not contradict his transferral of loyalty. If he had not fought, the others would have executed him. I can understand that. We require that of our operatives serving with the Sandinistas and Salvadorian guerrillas and the EGP in Guatemala. They must impress their compatriots with their fervor and accomplishments to remain effective agents for the International—even if they kill a few individuals who may or may not be ideologically sympathetic to our cause. It is a calculated and acceptable cost of operation.''

"But in the time since Mexico?''

Gunther thought a moment before answering. "Lyons explained that during interrogations. As an operative for his government, he assumed he would be under continual surveillance. His mail, his calls, his contacts. Any attempt to contact our representatives would have been observed, he told us. Even an odd move or variation in his routine would have aroused suspicion resulting in his seizure, interrogation and probable liquidation. So he did not attempt to contact us. He stated that he waited for us to contact him. He stated that his vacation to Guatemala had been his first effort to totally break away from the possible surveillance.''

"Did he attempt to make contact in my country?''

"He says he did not have the opportunity. Even the visit to Guatemala was not without risk, he believed. Therefore, he would visit a mercenary known to his superiors. The visit would provide a cover. And the circumstances would provide the opportunity for a contact.''

"Do you believe him?''

"I am, of course, assuming every word is a lie. I am proceeding as if he were a known infiltrator. The device—'' Gunther pointed to the one of the photos in Lyons's file "—allows us to monitor him and, if necessary, to terminate him at will. That is our ultimate guarantee of his loyalty. And if he is not loyal, the device allows us to limit our vulnerability.''

"But do you believe him?"

"The man confounds me. I am personally beginning to believe he actually wanted to join us when I encountered him in Mexico. He obviously enjoys luxury and women. He cooperated fully in the questioning. He talks of recruiting his friends so that their team can work together again. He seems to be dedicated not so much to his country or an ideology as his team. The man is either selling his soul or playing a very long game. And this man is not known for his patience.''

25

A line of three glowing dots transected the target.

Lyons had insisted on tritium nightsights. A gunsmith employed by the International had drilled two small holes on the leaf sight of the rifle, then another hole in the bead of the front sight. Insertion of the glowing isotope tritium had created self-powered, shock-proof and high-visibility sights usable even in total darkness.

Like the nightsight system employed on the Galil rifle, the three dots allowed Lyons to simply place the center dot of the front sight on the target, then line up the two rear dots.

No electronics. No batteries. No knobs to adjust. No phosphorus green scene moving with shadows to interpret. No worry about knocks to the circuitry or out-of-line scope mountings.

He was equipped with a .22 semiauto plinking rifle. A high-quality plinking rifle, but still a .22. Threatening the target with all of 150 foot-pounds of impact-shocking power.

The shot had to be exact. In one of the eyes or in the center of the forehead. If the bullet hit a cheek, the target suffered only a scar. If it hit off center in the forehead, a trip to the emergency room, perhaps a week in the hospital. Even a shot to the temple might not kill.

A 9 mm would have been better. Perhaps a subsonic cartridge loaded with a steel-cored slug. A slug designed to be mated with a full-power charge of powder and fired from a submachine gun. Instead of coming out at a speed of fifteen hundred feet per second, the steel-cored slug would move at one thousand or less. But when it hit, it would penetrate. Lead flattened. Lead slowed when it hit bone. Steel would punch through the skull and continue deep into the brain.

His partners on Able Team employed exactly that cartridge with their Beretta 93-R selective-fire auto-pistols. Loading the marvelous Berettas with subsonic cartridges and steel-cored slugs created a silent, one-hand submachine gun.

Lyons's personal weapon went one step further. Konzaki, the late, great weaponsmith, had redesigned, reengineered and hand-machined a Colt Government Model, incorporating the innovations of the Beretta auto-pistols. When he'd finished, the interior mechanisms of the Colt no longer resembled what Browning had invented and patented. Like on the Berettas, a fold-down lever and oversized trigger guard provided a positive two-hand grip. But it fired silent, full-powered .45 caliber slugs, in semiauto and 3-shot burst modes. With an extended 10-shot magazine loaded with hollowpoints, Lyons would face anything short of an armored personal carrier. That Colt—the Colt Frankenstein—did the job.

A form shifted. Lyons concentrated on the target, watching the target's movement, trying to anticipate the next move.

Flashes, and as the pistol reports came an instant later, Lyons fired once, then again as the target fell back.

Acceleration threw the rifle against the window-frame. Lyons pulled back the rifle and set the safety as the van sped away. Lyons braced himself for the turn. And exactly as the scenario dictated, the van whipped through a right turn.

But the estate grounds did not allow for the driver to rehearse the other turns. He slowed and coasted through three slow turns, then returned to the rehearsal area.

Lyons called out the window to the security men assisting him. "What's my score?"

"Come take a look...."

First, he dropped the magazine out of the rifle, then carefully eased back the action lever to clear the chamber. He snapped back the action several times to make absolutely sure. Getting out, he held the rifle with the muzzle pointed straight up. Even an absolutely unloaded .22-caliber rifle presented the threat of an accident.

In the glare of an improvised work light, the security men examined the molded clay head. The clay head had been mounted on a post that moved on an assembly of swivels and rollers. The swivels allowed the assistants to move head and post from side to side to simulate movement. The rollers allowed the post to move backward as it shifted.

As one of the security men popped a starting pistol several times, the other man had jerked a pull-pin. The moving, retreating target had then fallen backward, as if shot.

Lyons looked down at the molded head. The realistic features of the flesh-toned face now had two imperfections. One bullet had entered the tear duct of the left eye. The other bullet had hit in the center of the target's forehead, a finger width to the right.

"Shit, man, look at that."

"Damn fine shooting, specialist."

"Think so? I wanted to put one in each eye!"

His assistants laughed. One man said, "I declare this guy dead."

"Seriously, I aimed dead center on the bridge of his nose. I guess I can't do better than a two-inch spread with these glow-in-the-dark sights."

"Unless he's a pea-brain, you'll still kill him."

"And that's not counting the other bullets going into him from the pistol."

"Yeah," Lyons agreed. "But what if el pistolero don't shoot at all?"

"He'll have exact instructions."

"An exact maybe." Lyons pulled the head upright. "Put some makeup on this dead guy. This time, I'm going to try to put three in his face."

26

On a street of brownstones and expensive foreign cars, Lyons waited in the van. He did not know the street, or where in the District of Columbia the van had parked. He only knew that he waited to kill a man.

Two other men waited in the van with him. The driver sat behind the steering wheel, the head-phones of a personal stereo on his head. He bounced and swayed with the music he heard. His head jerked from side to side as he looked every-where in the street, glancing into the mirrors, looking into the windows overlooking the street.

Nerves, Lyons thought.

The other man sat at Lyons's side. Seeming to sleep, the man held a suppressor-equipped MAC-10 in his hands. He served as security. If pursued by guards or police during their getaway, he would provide firepower.

The subgunner also served as enforcer. If Lyons tried to turn the rifle on the other men and escape, he would not make it to freedom. Lyons knew it. The other men knew it. No one had to talk about it.

Peering out the van's rear window, Lyons kept his attention on the street. No one would see his ri-fle. The outswung window allowed him only a very narrow view, but the tinted window also blocked the sight of anyone looking at the van. An armrest bolted to the side wall allowed Lyons to effortlessly keep the rifle at his shoulder, the rifle aimed approximately where the target would appear.

He had practiced for this for a week. He could put three shots in a human forehead in a fraction of a second. In the narrow street, the reports would sound like echos of the robber's pistol.

Watching the steps where the target would appear, Lyons saw a form shift in a car window. No, a reflected form. He could not see the punk where he waited, but the reflection gave him away. Not too slick. If anyone walking on the predawn street or a patrolling police car spotted the punk, the assassination got canceled.

Then again, Lyons might cancel the assassination. When he saw the target, he would decide. His infiltration of the International had a higher social value. Balance a chance at a death strike on the International against the life of a newspaperman or a congressman or a drug boss cutting in the International's trade.

But if he recognized his target, if he saw a face in his sights of a man he could not kill, Lyons would kill the punk and try to break away from his partners in the van.

Thinking about it, he realized he would be taking a very serious risk to make a break. The enforcer an arm's distance away had orders to execute him if he attempted to escape. As did the driver.

Outside, Gunther had positioned a man to kill the pistol-punk as he ran. Why not Lyons? And how many other backup gunmen waited on the street?

More than a month before, on the mountain ridge in the Cuchumatanes, he had accepted death. Not surrendered. Accepted as a fact the distinct possibility of sudden death. Now he faced it again; now he stood at the door to the void.

Hey, friends, Lyons thought to himself. I'm one step away. Konzaki, Nate, my Xavante friends who didn't make it, you Quicheneros, Flor—all you warriors for...for what? For freedom. You who lost your lives for freedom, I'm close. Don't know how close, but I'm close....

The thought of Flor made Lyons smile. If she waited for him in a Norse afterlife or in a swirl of beauty around Huitzilopochli or as a spirit in the forever-flowering forest paradise of the Xavantes—sorry about all the women back at the estate. Just part of the job. Can't let Gunther think I'm not corrupted by the pretty girls and good times. He's got to think I want the fast life of an International gunslinger superstar.

"What's so funny?" the backup subgunner asked.

"What?" Lyons didn't take his eyes off the steps to the brownstone.

"You're laughing."

"Just joking with myself."

"Telling yourself jokes? You are a cool one, mister."

"Why not? What do I have to be nervous about? It's the guy who's coming out that door who's got the—he's coming!"

"Get that engine running!" the subgunner told the driver. Lyons watched a short, heavyset man in an overcoat kiss a woman in the doorway. In the porch light, he saw the man's gray hair and gray skin. The young woman's blond hair seemed to flame. The light shimmered on her satin robe. The woman stood half a head taller than her lover.

Old guy. Young woman. He's made a habit of spending most of the night at her place and Gunther spotted him.

The driver raced the van's engine. Lyons hissed to the subgunner. "Tell him to stop that! The truck's vibrating! It'll throw off my shots."

Relaying his command, the subgunner cursed the driver. "You dumb shit! What's with you? You popping those whites again? On a job? You crazy?"

Lyons concentrated on his target. The distinguished gray-haired man came down the steps one at a time, turning twice or three times to look back at the woman.

The punk appeared. Lyons saw the error immediately. The height of the punk matched the height of the target. And the punk jittered, bounced on his feet, moving back and forth, his head eclipsing the face of the wide-eyed man. Lyons saw the punk wave the pistol.

He heard the young woman screaming, her shrieks echoing in the street, as he muttered, "Shit! Shit! Shit! Who planned this shit! That old fuck is short. Why didn't they get a midget mugger?"

And he exhaled to calm himself. The three glowing dots transected the face of the target, the center dot giving the old man a luminous third eye.

The pistol fired and the jittering punk jumped sideways and Lyons fired simultaneously. Two high-velocity jacketed solid slugs punched into the back of the punk's head.

"What the fuck!" Lyons cursed as the van screeched away. As in the rehearsals, the van powered through a hard right turn.

"Oh, shit..." The subgunner sighed. "Gunther is going to do it to us."

"He jumped sideways!" Lyons banged the side of the van with his hand, acting out a scene of frustration. All that moral equivocation, all that practice and waiting—he decides to shoot that old man and the street punk jumps into the bullets. "I cannot believe this."

"Believe it, mister. I saw it. Perfect shooting, but the wetback put his head in the way. That senator's going to be wondering who the hell saved him."

The van hurtled throught the streets, the wheels pounding on potholes and texture. The driver powered through a wide left turn, the van tilting far to the right.

"Senator?"

"Hey!" The subgunner shouted forward to the driver. "Cool it! What's with you?"

"Slow down!" Lyons told the driver. "We're gone already. You're going to get us stopped by the cops."

"Lights behind us—" The driver whipped through another turn, the tires sideslipping.

Lyons looked back. He saw no traffic on the predawn street. "What lights?"

"Cops everywhere!" The driver wailed.

"He's flying on meth, the stupid—"

Glancing off a parked car, careening across the street to sideswipe a line of other parked cars, the van hit the curb and rolled.

Chaos, screaming metal, impact. Lyons kicked the van's back doors open. Stumbling out, he looked back and saw the back wheels straight up and spinning. But the front wheels had folded into the van. He heard a man screaming. Lyons crawled back into the van.

The interior stank of gasoline. Lyons found a jacket and pulled, and the subgunner crawled free of the wreck. Staggering, dizzy from his own shock, Lyons managed to get around the van to the front.

Tangled metal held the driver. Wailing and babbling, the driver stared around him, not comprehending his injuries. Lyons jerked at the jammed door, then reached inside, examining the driver's injuries by touch. He found blood and steel.

"Leave that shithead!" the subgunner told him. "He's high—he popped pills for this job and that's why we're fucked. Leave him."

"We can't!" Lyons said. "We leave him, we compromise the action."

"We can leave him!" Grabbing Lyons's arm and spinning him away, the subgunner took a lighter from his pocket. He flicked on the flame and showed it to the driver. "This is what you get, understand?"

"Noooooooooooooo!"

And the subgunner reached into the wreck and touched the dripping gasoline.

27

Gadgets and Blancanales rushed from the elevator. Seeing them, the tall, gray-suited man in the foyer put away his walkie-talkie. He nodded to the other conservatively dressed men standing in the hospital's white corridor before turning to the two men of Able Team and extending his hand.

"Fernworth," he introduced himself.

"Rosario, and my friend the Wizard."

"Why they call you Wizard?"

"'Cause of all the wonderful things I do— Where's this Mexican or Central American whatever? You know, the crispy critter?"

"Ugly way to describe it, but it's accurate." Fernworth led them down the corridor. "Ninety percent burns. He won't live very long, but—"

"But he's talking," Blancanales interrupted. "What else had he said about our partner?"

"Enough to identify him. Even the name, Lyons."

"All right!" Gadgets exclaimed. "Fantastic! First lead we've gotten."

"I don't know if you should celebrate. Your partner's involved in an attempted assassination."

"Hey, agent," Gadgets corrected the man. "News I got indicated Lyons is still on the side of truth, justice and the American way."

"That remains to be determined." Another agent spoke. Grayer, older, he commanded the group of plainclothes men. His eyes had web-works of black lines, the marks of years of long days and worry for the safety of elected representatives. "From what the man has told us, your friend intended to kill the senator. I interviewed the witnesses, and what they told me is that the Salvadorian lurched to one side at precisely the wrong moment. Lurched into the line of fire. He accidentally took the bullets intended for the senator. As of this moment, your Mr. Lyons is a federal fugitive."

"Yeah?" Gadgets laughed. "Betcha he's shaking in his—" '

Blancanales cut off his partner. "Sir, can we question the man in there?"

"In my presence. With the federal prosecutor as a witness and a tape recorder running. You do realize you may be contributing to the case against your associate?"

"I very seriously doubt if he's guilty of any crime," Blancanales answered.

"Hey, I know," Gadgets told the senior officer. "My news indicates—"

"Hearsay and fragmentary information," the gray man interrupted. "Your information means nothing in this investigation—"

Gadgets raised his voice to speak over him. "Don't tell me that! I know for sure Lyons is still with us. Allow me to elaborate. Listen! To be precise, my news was that the pistol man—the Mexi-

can or Central American, whoever—got two bullets
in the back of the head.''

"True—''

"Then there it is! That tells me that my partner's still on our side.''

"A screwup, nothing! If Lyons meant to hit that
senator, those two bullets would've been in that
senator's head, understand me? Now let's go in
there. We got some questions to ask that creep.''

28

"I never went on a more amateurish action!" Lyons screamed across the desk at Colonel Gunther. "Why didn't anyone think of the height of that senator? That jerk stood about five foot four. So you went and found a junkie exactly five foot four. Didn't anyone think about that?"

His hands folded, Jon Gunther listened to Lyons's tirade. He watched the ex-cop, ex-antiterrorist fighter pace the office. He finally asked the obvious, "Why didn't you think of it?"

Rage making his jaw muscles stand out, Lyons glared at the officer of the International. "Because you would not tell me who I was shooting. Because you had the distance measured to the inch. Because you had every other detail down, every other detail but the one that counted. You won't let me work on the planning, then you ask me why I didn't anticipate the problem. Too much. Let me tell you this, colonel. I don't like amateur hour on television, I don't like amateur hour on actions. Next time, I plan it all, or I don't do it. All right?"

Gunther said nothing for a moment. His steel-blue eyes studied Lyons. Then he said simply, "Agreed."

"What?"

"Agreed. On your next mission, to the extent possible, you will have the responsibility of planning. And you begin planning that mission immediately."

"What mission?"

"You have experience in Nicaragua. We will be exploiting your experience."

"Who do I shoot? President Ortega?"

"No. Archbishop Obando."

Lyons did not speak for a moment. He saw the simplicity of fact.

If he succeeded, Nicaragua and the world would assume the Sandinistas had murdered the leader of the church. No matter what the Sandinistas denied, the Catholic faithful of Nicaragua and the surrounding nations would attack the Marxists as never before, and the Sandinistas would know they had not killed the archbishop.

If he failed to assassinate Obando—or if he succeeded, and the Sandinista security forces killed or captured Lyons, they would display the blond *norteamericano* and denounce the United States. Which would turn the screws of confrontation tighter and tighter. The United States government would, of course, deny any role in the assassination or the attempted assassination. The Contras in Honduras and Costa Rica would assume the Sandinistas had fabricated the plot to discredit the non-Marxist opposition. Everyone would believe what they wanted.

No matter what, succeed or fail, whether the archbishop lived or died, or if Lyons lived or died, the attempt would enflame the region.

This is it, Lyons realized. The other night, waiting to kill the man who came down the steps from the brownstone, he had resolved to make the decision to kill or die when he knew the identity of his target. Gunther had just told him the name of a man Lyons would not kill. Even if it meant Lyons died.

But Lyons would play along. The forest of the Honduras-Nicaragua border would be a great place for an escape—if he didn't get the opportunity sooner.

"Oh, wow! You want a war? That's what you get. When do you want him hit?"

"You have no objections to assassinating the archbishop?" Gunther asked.

"Why?" was Lyons's only reply.

29

As the pilot held the Piper in a wide circle, Blancanales and Gadgets studied the estate with binoculars.

They had questioned the badly burned driver until he had died. Though the security personnel of the International had taken precautions to keep the driver ignorant of the location of the estate—never allowing him to drive from the estate to the District of Columbia, shuttling him back and forth in a closed car—the driver knew the value of information. He had memorized the twists and turns of the roads, then traced his route on a highway map. The driver thought information on the International would be valuable if he needed to plea-bargain with a prosecutor.

He didn't get the chance. He stopped breathing only twelve hours after the crash. But as far as the official records went, he had died in the flaming van.

Now the two men of Able Team scanned the International base. They saw that the landscaping and forests concealed concentric circles of defense.

An outer perimeter of chain link was backed by a patrol road.

Set between the outer perimeter and the inner fence was a forest screening the estate from observers.

A high wrought-iron fence was interspaced with guard positions. Roads and walkways provided access to vehicles and patrols.

Then, on the roofs of the multistory buildings, were more guard positions.

"Look at all that money," Gadgets said, shaking his head. "I know they must've spent millions on tricks. There's got to be a catalog of electronics down there. Sensors, video, infrared, ultrahigh frequency, dogs, attack-trained cats, eye-eating sparrows—"

"Don't let your imagination go crazy, Wizard. We've hit worse."

"I don't know about that. With this place, if we put together enough firepower to punch through all that...they'd probably call the police."

The pilot laughed. He looked back to them. "Thought you spooks were fearless."

Gadgets gave Blancanales a glance. "I tell a joke and someone takes me serious. Just drive, will you?"

"Yes, sir! How about we go in lower for a look? Maybe trim some of their trees? You won't have to use those binoculars. Unless maybe you think they'll report us to the FAA."

With his binoculars locked in on a guardhouse next to the gate, Gadgets commented to his partner, "Bet they have LAW rockets in there."

"And M-60s on the buildings," Blancanales added.

"Taking it up to ten thousand feet," the pilot joked.

Studying the estate, Gadgets snapping telephoto pictures, they completed several circles before flying back toward Baltimore. Blancanales scanned the countryside with his binoculars, Gadgets jotted down notes. The pilot stayed quiet, allowing his passengers to think. Gadgets finally broke the silence: "I don't think we can just drive up and say we're plumbers."

"You're right. No easy way this time."

"I got it!" Gadgets slapped his hands together. He folded up his notes with finality.

"What?" Blancanales demanded.

Gadgets glanced at the back of the pilot's head and mouthed the word "Wait."

30

Carl Lyons had taken a conference room for his planning of the assassination of the archbishop of Nicaragua. There, the double doors locked to keep out Cheryl, Luisa, Jeanie or Barbara, he pinned maps to the walls and spread photos over the long committee tables. He used the telephone to order information and meals. Papers and books stood piled beside the table.

Nights, he slept on the carpeted floor. He had overdosed on the pleasures of the hydro-therapy room and vibro-beds and midnight rolls on the lawn. He had an action to plan.

He had begun by reviewing everything published in English on the duties, routes and idiosyncrasies of the archbishop. After a few days of reading, Lyons had the archbishop's travels sketched on a map of Nicaragua. He also indicated the location of the old man's house in Managua, then drafted a map showing the street he traveled during his normal working day.

No single plan could anticipate every contingency. If the agit-prop mobs of the Sandinistas forced the archbishop to cancel a tour of the villages, Lyons did not want to wait a month for the next scheduled tour. If rain forced the archbishop

to cancel an appearance at one location, Lyons
would know the alternative assembly place.

Lyons wanted to prove his intention to make the
kill. When he presented his plans to Gunther for
review and criticism, Gunther would see viable
scenarios.

But Lyons would not murder the archbishop.

He wanted to present plans so detailed and exact
that Gunther would not hesitate to commit the men
and equipment to the action.

A quickly sketched scenario called for Lyons and
a number of backup men to land at a Contra air-
field in Honduras, then cross the border. There,
they would march only so far as the nearest Sandinista strong point and capture uniforms and vehicles. Forged papers would be their key to deep
penetration of Nicaragua. Finally, in the center of
the nation, they would wait for the opportunity to
execute one of Lyons's several scenarios.

All of the scenarios included escape plans and
routes. Professionals are not suicidal. He did not
want Gunther to doubt his professionalism.

Or his commitment to the mission.

Because his commitment would go no further
than the Nicaraguan border.

When Lyons crossed the border, he became a free
man.

With a weapon in his hands, good boots and a
compass, he would evade his unit. If they pursued
him, they risked encountering Sandinistan coun-
terinsurgent teams. Moving alone, Lyons knew he
could evade the International and the Sandinistas.
No one could catch him. If he ran alone....

Gunther had captured him in Guatemala because of a combination of factors. The women and children. The multiple ambushes. The helicopters. The one road to Huehuetenango. The civil patrols. Gunther leading the pursuit. All the factors had worked against Lyons.

The next pursuit would be different. This time, Lyons would escape to freedom.

But first, Lyons had to give the appearance of wholehearted devotion to the mission. That would give him the element of surprise when he crossed the border.

So he drew diagrams, traced the diagrams onto maps of Managua, then studied high-altitude photos and drew lines of fire onto the photos.

Lyons had one dread. That after he finished, after he escaped, Gunther would use the scenarios to mount another assassination mission. But he had to accept that risk. If he left one detail out, if he allowed a distance or an angle or time to flaw his plans, he knew Gunther could discover the flaw. Gunther knew his business. And if Gunther found a deliberate flaw, Gunther would guess Lyons's true plans. Therefore, the plans had to be real.

Knocking on the double door interrupted his work. "What?"

"Hey, specialist!" A woman's voice shouted. "It's party time!"

"Can't. I'm working."

"You've been working for days. Take a break. Or we'll break in."

"Who's we?"

"Me, Jeanie."

"And Luisa. Tonight's party night!"

Luisa, the young lady from Brooklyn with the soft, womanly body and the hot mouth.

Jeanie, a white-skinned redhead, skin so white that blue veins showed through everywhere, her small-breasted body so delicate he thought he would crush her in bed. But she had surprised him with her passion and endurance, that white skin concealing a pelvis with the power of a two-ton cam.

Why had they interrupted him?

All the women in the facility—nurses, therapists, technicians, receptionists—worked for the International. Everything they did, they did at Gunther's command. Gunther had decided to stop the interrogation by drugs and shock torture. Gunther had decided to use the women to quiz Lyons. Whether a technician used high-voltage cattle prod or opium, sinsemillian, or sex, it was all the same. Interrogation and control.

If the women interrupted him, they interrupted him at Gunther's orders.

Play along. If Gunther wanted him out of the conference room for the night, Lyons would go. Let Gunther send in a search unit. Let them study his notes and maps and drawings. Let them wire a microphone or install a video camera. What would Gunther learn?

Exactly what Lyons would present to Gunther in a few days. A professional and meticulously planned mission—to assassinate the archbishop of Nicaragua. Incorporating several distinct options.

Quitting his drawing, Lyons left the pencil on the paper and went to the door. He decided to maintain his pretense of secrecy. He opened the door and stepped into the corridor, locking the door behind him.

"All right. What's the occasion?"

"What're you doing in there?" Luisa asked. Her breath smelled of liquor. She tired to push the door open. "You've been in there for days."

"¡Nadie pasaran!"

"What does that mean?"

"No one goes in there."

"You got secrets from us?" Jeanie asked. Her fragile white hand grabbed his shirt. She tried to make a menacing face. "What's the secret, specialist?"

"You want in on it? Go see Colonel Gunther and volunteer for fieldwork."

"Oh..." Lusia held the vowel and nodded, her lips a glistening circle of red with lipstick. "...that kind of secret. No thanks. We take care of guys who get wounded doing fieldwork. No thanks. I want to walk on real legs all my life. No plastic legs for me."

"You'll be going out again?" Jeanie hugged Lyons and put her head against his chest. "Will it be dangerous? I'll be so good to you. You'll never want to leave."

"Hey, you!" Luisa feigned jealousy. "Don't make a play for my man in front of me."

Lyons almost laughed.

"So what's wrong?" Jeanie asked. "Why are you so quiet? Are your worried about your job?"

Lyons smiled. "You've been so good to me already." He saw Luisa give him a sharp look. "I mean, everyone has given me such loving care. I thought I'd died and gone to heaven. You know, like the heaven they had for the assassins—the hashshāshin.''

Luisa laughed. ''It's not like it's hard work. You are a good time, Mr. Specialist.''

''So what about this party?''

''All the officers and department heads are going to the reception,'' Jeanie told him. ''With Mr. Unomundo himself and some politicians and all these foreigners. They'll be over in the main building. Didn't you hear the helicopters?''

''No. There's no windows in that conference room. We're not invited to the party, right?''

''Us? We just work here. We're having our own party. All the night staff—you know, the girls, the technicians, some patients. It'll be a good time.''

''Technicians? You mean the assholes who specialize in high-voltage questions? Yeah, I want to party with those guys. Me and my chain saw.''

''They're not bad guys,'' Jeanie protested. ''They just take their orders and do their job. Just like you. Besides they think you're cool. You took the treatment and didn't break down. All that time. Why don't you just shake hands with them and say it's cool. I mean, you'd do the same if you got the orders, right?''

Wrong. Lyons wanted to explain the difference between a fighter and a torturer. But he had a role to play. ''Yeah, you're right. In fact, I guess I've done a lot worse.''

''See?'' Jeanie pulled him away from the door. ''Come on. Can you play the drums? We need a drummer for the band.''

31

Cutting the power to the two-cycle engine, Gadgets suddenly flew in silence. He heard only the rushing of the night over the plastic wings of the ultralight plane. Some of the cables and fiberglass struts hummed with the slipwind.

A few hundred yards behind him and to his right, he heard the popping of Blancanales's engine. Gadgets looked back. The batlike shape of the second ultralight cut across the stars. Then the engine noise cut off.

They started their glide down to the distant lights of the International facility. Gadgets touched the pedal controls to take his line of flight to the south of the estate. Their plan included a flyby before landing.

This mission would be a hard assault. They knew they faced strong opposition and they intended to destroy the facility, whether they found Lyons or not.

Revenge or liberation.

For this mission, both Gadgets and Blancanales had abandoned their standard weapons in favor of heavy assault weaponry. Instead of a short, lightweight CAR, Gadgets had a M-249 squad automatic weapon. The 5.56 mm machine guns had been modified for this action. First, they had shortened the barrels, cutting off the six inches in front of the sights and gas tubes and refitting the flash supressors. The bipod legs had been removed. Other parts—the aluminum tubing of the skeleton stock, the stamped steel receiver, most of the stamped steel operating parts—had been remanufactured with titanium. Loaded with lightweight plastic magazines containing two hundred belt-linked rounds of 5.56 SS-109 ammunition, the abbreviated weapons weighed only eighteen pounds. This allowed the two men to carry four more plastic magazines of ammunition, for a total of one thousand rounds of alternating armor-piercing and tracers, two steel-tipped rounds to one tracer—a custom mix for the night's combat.

They also carried their silenced Beretta 93-R pistols and clusters of MU-50G controlled-effect grenades for room clearing.

To multiply the confusion and destruction of their assault, the ultralight craft had bomb racks fitted to the frames. The racks held thirty stun-flash antiterrorist grenades fitted with radio-triggered fuses. As Gadgets and Blancanales circled the estate, they would dump the small grenades along the perimeter. Later, they would pop the grenades to create the illusion of an assault on the perimeter fences.

Revenge or liberation. Either way, they intended to waste the Virginia installation.

Gadgets munched on a Twinkie as he watched the distant lights of the buildings and perimeter fences. The lights formed a cluster within two circles, like a target with a diffused center. Headlights streaked along the country road leading to the estate.

Their information indicated a diplomatic reception that night. Gadgets and Blancanales did not care. Let the world think the chic crowd had been the victims of terrorism. The diplomats, the foreign colonels, the wealthy expatriates—they had financed and coordinated decades of horror against the common people of their nations.

Tonight, death came to the elite.

32

Marijuana and opium smoke clouding into the corridor, Lyons staggered from the cafeteria. He held a bottle of Chivas Regal by the neck and he raised the bottle to his mouth. His throat moved with gulps.

But he swallowed nothing. Lurching to the far wall, Lyons braced himself. He glanced behind him. No one had followed him out.

What fun, meeting the goons who tried to fry me. Sadists aren't bad guys, they just like to hurt people.

But now he would turn the party to his advantage. He assumed Gunther had sent a team to search his planning room. So he would use tonight to search some of the other offices.

No one came from the cafeteria. Lyons staggered away, pretending to be drunk. He did not need to pretend much. With everyone in the cafeteria smoking various drugs, to breathe meant drug intoxication.

Though Lyons did not let the drugs and alcohol dull his battle-honed reflexes, he faked a weaving walk, bouncing from wall to wall, spilling his Chivas as he wandered toward the office corridor.

He knew where the security detail hid their set of emergency keys. Pausing at the corner, he listened. He heard nothing, no voices, no movement, no static bursts from walkie-talkies.

Looking around, he saw no one at the desk and he walked quickly over. He reached to the top of the video monitors viewing the entrances to the wing, and found the desk key by touch. Part luck, part educated guess. Seconds later he had opened the bottom drawer and taken out the ring of keys.

Moving fast, he went to the line of office doors. Which office first?

One door he had never seen open, so he opened it first and slipped in. He stood in the darkness, listening.

He heard a faint whirring and squeaking. And a steady beat, like a heartbeat. Lyons listened.

A heartbeat. And a background rushing sound. Breathing.

He switched on the light. He saw a bank of electronic units, including a turning reel-to-reel recorder. Folders lay on the desk. A light box had been mounted to one wall. An X ray hung on the light box.

The sounds came from an audio monitor.

Whispering to himself, he said, "What do we have—"

And he heard the words come from the monitor.

Startled, Lyons stared at the monitor a moment. He looked at the turning reels of the recorders. Unconsciously, he swallowed and he heard the sound from the monitor. He cleared his throat. The monitor simplified the slight cough. He rubbed his hand across the beard stubble on his throat and he heard a scratchy sound come from the monitor.

Lyons went to the desk. He glanced at the light box and noticed that the X ray had the name C. Lyons scratched on the print. He switched on the light.

The X ray showed his skull and the vertebrae of his neck. He recognized the fillings in his molars.

He did not recognize the shadow of the device in his throat. Peering at it, he saw nothing to allow him to guess its purpose. But as he rubbed the scar on his throat he heard the scratchy sound from the audio monitor.

A microphone.

And what else?

Lyons pulled out the notebooks standing on the desk. He flipped through one, finding notes on his conduct since his release from the interrogation cells. He noticed summaries dictated by the various women he had slept with in that time. That came as no surprise. He closed that notebook.

The next folder contained close-up shots of a strange device. The outlines matched the shadow on the X ray.

A series of pages showed a sun-scarred campesino strapped into a straight-backed wooden chair. The chair sat in a courtyard somewhere. Lyons saw a whitewashed wall and splash of tropical flowers.

He also saw a line of sutures on the old man's throat, in exactly the same place as the scar on his own throat.

Turning the page, Lyons saw a spray of blood from the throat of the campesino. The head went at a right angle to the neck, the ragged ends of flesh and bronchial tubes extended from the ruin of his neck.

Now Lyons knew why Gunther had given Lyons conditional freedom. If Lyons outwitted or over-powered the few guards surrounding him, he would not run far before a trigger impulse took off his head.

Frantic, Lyons searched through the other note-books. How could he disarm the object in his throat? How could he remove the death device?

The intercom phone buzzed. He watched lights blink on and off as someone tried to reach a num-ber. Finally one light stayed on. Lyons picked up the receiver and held his hand over the mouth-piece. He heard Cheryl's voice:

"The specialist left the party and didn't come back."

"He go toward the conference room?"

"Don't know. We didn't see him go."

"We'll keep him out of the area. Thanks."

As Cheryl and the security man hung up, Lyons broke the connection. They would block the corri-dor of the conference room first, then they would sweep the general area.

How much more time could he give the search for information? He saw the lights on the intercom phone flashing as the security man alerted the other stations.

No more time. He quickly returned the folders and notebooks to the previous order. Taking his bottle, he turned off the light and chanced a look outside. No one was in the corridor. The security men would be in another wing of the building.

Moving fast, he relocked the office, then returned the keys to their drawer. He poured Chivas down his sweatshirt and hurried back toward the cafeteria. When he saw the blazer-coated security man, he held up the bottle. "Hey, man! Coming to the party?"

33

At approximately thirty-three miles per hour, Gadgets silently circled the estate, his black-winged ultralight like a shadow against the stars. He saw limousines and luxury cars parked in front of a central building. Lights blazed everywhere. He saw two-man patrols walking the paths.

He heard a dance band, the music coming to him in moments as he passed one building after another. The peaceful grounds revolved beneath him.

Like a park. Like prom night. All the ladies in the de la Renta gowns. All the gents in their black tuxes and bow ties. All your millions. All your goon-squad security. No big deal. Things would change quick.

Gadgets raised his hand-radio and gave his partner a code: "Doing it, nine o'clock to three o'clock."

As Gadgets neared the main entrance gate, he pivoted the mechanical safety on the drop mechanism. Gliding over the road, he turned the crank one click to release the first sun-flash grenade. He heard it cut throught the branch of a tree. He held the easy circle and continued dropping the small black canisters onto the lawns and flower beds.

"All down," he radioed Blancanales. "Ready?"

"Ready."

"Going in."

Pointing his ultralight for the building most distant from the limousines and bright lights, Gadgets slap-checked his weapons and gear. It did not matter to him if he made an unobserved landing. So what if they spotted the ultralight coming in?

If they did not kill him in the first three seconds, he would be out and killing them.

The photos of the estate had given them the location of a perfect landing strip. A band of lawn, hundreds of yards long and fifty yards wide, ran parallel to the satellite building. The aerial photos showed guard positions on the roof of that building but they had brought a special treat just for those emplacements.

The immaculate lawn rushed toward him, and he aimed the small plane between two stands of trees. Three seconds...

He hit the flaps and the wheels touched. Wings flexing with the impact, he bounced and skidded across the lawn. He coasted the ultralight to a side-slipping stop.

Jerking his harness and cargo buckles open, Gadgets did not stop to look for response. He moved. Grunting with the weight of the munitions he carried, he ran from the ultralight with his shorty M-249 and a duffel bag of LAW rockets in the other. He threw himself flat in the night shadow beneath a tree and jerked out the first fiberglass rocket tube.

No shouting. No firing. No movement on the grounds or on the roof overlooking him. But that did not mean they had not seen him. The sentries could have their rifles on him now, waiting for authorization to execute the intruder.

Behind him, he heard the soft rushing sound of the second ultralight coming down, then the squeaking and fluttering of the plastics during the landing. Gadgets heard his hand-radio buzz an instant later:

"You see anything?" Blancanales asked.

"*Nada*. But we hit them, anyway," Gadgets replied.

"On the count of ten..."

Mentally counting off the seconds, Gadgets extended the fiberglass tube to arm the rocket and sighted on the outline of the guard post. On the count of ten, rockets flashed from the ground and the two emplacements disappeared in sprays of flame and fragments. The explosions echoed from the distant buildings. They did not wait for response before moving.

Gadgets looped the strap of his bag of remaining rockets over his shoulder and staggered out, his M-249 in his hands, his finger alongside the trigger. He saw the black suited, bulky silhouette of Blancanales to his left.

There was a movement to his right, and Gadgets fired from the hip, the first tracer going high over the form, the second 5-shot burst throwing the man back. Gadgets touched the trigger once again, and the 3-shot burst—two armor-piercing and one tracer—passing through the falling man's body.

Blancanales fired and someone screamed. Gadgets kept his eyes sweeping the area in front of him. A weapon flashed and a pistol slug thumped into his Kevlar body armor. Gadgets did not break stride as he put bursts into the darkness concealing the gunman. No more firing came.

Headlights bounced across the lawn toward them as several security vehicles converged on the intruders.

All right, Gadgets thought, gaining the cover of a doorway. Now the shit hits...

34

One leg thrown over his shoulder, Cheryl gasped and shrieked as Lyons hammered her against the door, his hands gripping her waist, forcing her body down hard on him. Smoke from her hashish and sensimillian cigar clouded around him. From time to time, Cheryl sucked down a long drag of the narcotic smoke. Lyons had refused to share it with her, so she repeatedly clamped her mouth over Lyons and forced the smoke into his lungs as he continued thrusting into her.

Ex-cop or not, she got Lyons stoned. Dizzy, seeing halos of colors on the blond woman's shadowed face, Lyons did not break their clutch. The music and laughter of the party continued at the far end of the corridor. Someone called out and then laughed when they saw the lovers up against the door.

As Cheryl shrieked again, Lyons thought he heard a double boom. The door banging, he thought, the party, whatever. Then he heard the high cyclic rate popping. Auto fire? Impossible. The jerks at the party must've turned on a video player. They liked to watch *Apocalypse Now* on the wide-screen projector and shoot the Vietnamese with rubber bands.

The door jerked open and Lyons and Cheryl fell back, hard, Cheryl shrieking a last time, her cry cutting off as she cracked her head on the linoleum.

Lyons looked up at Gadgets Schwarz.

Looking down at the pretty blond woman, her skirt around her waist, her open blouse revealing one breast, a smoking narcotic cigar in her hand, Gadgets tried to speak. His mouth moved as he looked from his long-lost partner to the unconscious woman.

Lyons communicated first. He did not speak. He put his hand over his mouth, than made an X sign and pointed at Gadgets and made another X sign.

Gadgets nodded. As he took out his hand-radio, Lyons pointed to the corner of the building. He motioned Gadgets to go there before speaking. Gadgets nodded again, though he did not understand. As he whispered into the hand-radio, Lyons got up, pulling up his pants. He pulled the door closed behind him and used Cheryl's clothes to tie her hands and ankles and to wrap a gag around her mouth.

Returning, Gadgets grinned at Lyons but said nothing. Lyons put his head back and pointed at the scar on his throat. He touched his lips and his ears, then pointed into the building.

Gadgets understood. He pointed to his hand-radio, then to Lyons's scar. Lyons nodded. Then Lyons pointed to one of the small grenades hooked to Gadgets's web gear, then to the scar on his throat again.

Oh, shit, Gadgets said silently.

Pistols and rifles fired, and an instant later, a pop silenced the fascist small-arms fire. They heard a

long, tearing burst from an M-249, the impact of
the slugs hammering walls and furniture. Seconds
later, Blancanales joined them.

"Lyons."

Jumping across the step separating them, banging equipment, Gadgets put his hand over Blancanales's mouth. Then leaning against his partner,
cupping both hands over his ear, he whispered:
"He says he's got a minimike in his throat, a transmitter of some kind. And it has an explosive
capability."

Blancanales looked at Lyons. With his hands,
Lyons mimed his throat exploding.

The three men of Able Team, finally reunited,
looked at one another, perplexed. Blancanales
summarized their dilemma by raising his hands,
open, the palms up, in a gesture of helplessness.

Lights approached. Blancanales braced his M-
249 against the side of the entry and put a burst
through the windshield of a security car, the headlights veering to one side as the driverless car drifted
across the lawn.

Lyons knew what he had to do. Reaching to
Gadgets's web gear, he tore off a plastic-wrapped
field dressing.

Understanding, Gadgets offered Lyons a razor-
sharp knife. Lyons shook his head, no.

He feared ferro-magnetic triggering of the
charge. The designers of the device knew that X
rays would reveal the placement of the device. With
the foreign object so close under the skin, a man
might be tempted to cut it out. Lyons assumed the
designers had countered this threat to the place-

ment by allowing the contact of a blade to trigger the charge. But he had to risk cutting it out.

Therefore, he would not use steel.

Rushing into the corridor, he went to the door of one of the private hospital rooms. Down the corridor, he saw only darkness and swirling smoke coming from the cafeteria. Blancanales had pooped the party.

Lyons kicked down the room's door. He rushed into the bath. Like a hotel, the sink had a sparkling tumbler. Holding the glass tumbler in his hand, looking at himself in the mirror, he calmed his breathing. The hashish and marijuana from Cheryl's cigar made him strangely distant from the scene, as if he looked at a full-size photo of himself, rather than his reflection.

No more time to waste. He tapped the tumbler against the edge of the sink, breaking it, then hit it again to shatter what remained. He selected three long slivers of glass and set them aside.

He took a moment to study the position of the scar and the lump under the surface in relationship to his carotid artery. They had put the device between the artery and the trachea. He risked bleeding to death if he slipped.

Putting a point of glass against the welt of his scar, Lyons took a breath—perhaps his last—and cut. Blood flowed down his neck. Pain came but he concentrated on the cut. Watching his hand in the mirror, he reopened the entire scar. He used his left hand to spread the flesh. Then he cut again, pressing harder, risking a wound to his trachea as he used the sliver of glass to probe for the device.

The glass touched something. Lyons expected the black flash of death, but nothing happened. He slid the blade of glass along the slick form buried in his flesh.

He heard a sound to his side. Blancanales watched him, astonishment and sympathy on his face. The ex-medic took one of the glass slivers from the sink and motioned for Lyons to lean back his head.

Lyons shook his head. Too much danger. If it popped, his friend would lose his hands. But Blancanales refused to consider the danger.

Turning Lyons, Blancanales had him sit on the sink, then bent back his head, putting the bleeding wound directly under the mirror's light. Lyons felt the glass blade in his friend's hand slice flesh.

Blancanales reached into the gaping wound with his fingers. Lyons felt the glass cutting him and suppressed his reflex to jerk away.

An instant later, Blancanales showed him a gleaming steel rod the size of an AAA battery. Then he dropped it in the toilet and flushed it.

"Got any other unidentified objects embedded in you?" Blancanales asked, slapping a field dressing over Lyons's wound.

"I hope not—"

"Better not." Blancanales knotted the dressing. "We don't have time to X-ray you. Here, take this. It is time to get out of here."

He passed the strap of the canvas case holding two LAW rockets to Lyons. They rushed out of the hospital room.

"Unomundo's here tonight. We've got to hit him—"

"No. We came to get you out. Fight until we found you, but now we got you it's time to get out."

At the entry, Gadgets lay prone, hitting targets of opportunity, firing lines of tracers at the headlights of converging security vehicles.

"You got it out?" Gadgets asked. "Fantastic. Now it's time to do some serious killing. Wipe out these pesky Nazis. Payback without end."

Blancanales fired an accurate burst into a form a hundred yards away. "Time to withdraw. The mission is accomplished as far as..."

"Withdraw where?" Gadgets demanded. "Take a look! We're surrounded! Nazis everywhere...."

Headlights ringed the perimeter. The throb of a helicopter passed overhead. Gadgets turned onto his back and fired his machine gun straight up into the belly of the aircraft. Rotors jamming, the helicopter fell straight down and shattered on the lawn.

An instant later, a woman in a flashing silver gown stumbled from the wreckage, a man in a tuxedo a step behind her. The man raised a pistol and it popped, two bullets pinging into the building.

Gadgets cut down both the survivors. "It's raining Nazis! So you tell me, Pol, which way out?"

"It would be suicide to—"

"That's what they'll think," Lyons countered as he pulled the second satchel of LAW rockets from Gadgets. "I say we hit the center, kill Unomundo, then get out in the confusion, that's the only—"

"Make maximum chaos!" Gadgets shouted over the firing of his M-249.

"Chaos to the max!" Lyons cut from the doorway, diving, crawling throught the flower beds as inaccurate return fire pocked the building. He heard shouts and pistol fire in the distance as the security men organized a counterstrike against the intruders. But from the other direction, he heard the throbbing of helicopters.

Lying prone in the flowers, Lyons saw another helicopter rising from the roof of the parking structure. He took out a LAW rocket and extended the tube. Sighting above the helicopter, he waited until he head the turbines shriek, then he fired.

As the helicopter rose straight up, the rocket caught it dead center. The warhead flashed, and the wildly spinning, flame-spraying wreck fell to the landing pad. The entire sky glowed orange as fuel splashed from ruptured fuel tanks and ignited.

A fire-shrouded helicopter attempted to escape the conflagration, but veered out of control, banking hard to one side, too hard, the fuselage going sideways. A rotor caught the edge of the structure and the helicopter cartwheeled through the night, disappearing behind the central building of the estate.

Screaming metal and screaming voices tore the night as flames blossomed and the entire area between the estate's center and the concrete parking structure glowed orange from burning fuel. Flames and black smoke swirled upward.

But the flash of the rocket tube had given away Lyons's position, and pistol rounds now zipped over him. And from the roof of a four-story building, a heavy machine gun flashed, the 7.62 mm slugs thumping into the lawn, and sparking off the walkway as the gunner tried to kill the intruder with the rockets.

Lyons broke the seals on another rocket and aimed. He put the rocket into a window immediately below the guard post and the entire emplacement flew into the air, the roof and walls spinning outward.

Auto fire came from the perimeter, the slugs shattering windows, whining off the building as the security force searched for the attackers with high-velocity bullets. Machine-gun fire answered the rifles.

"Okay, okay!" Blancanales answered. "Through the center and out."

A careening four-wheel drive truck spun onto the scene, rifles flashing from the windows. But Gadgets and Blancanales had the soft-steel vehicle outgunned. Two lines of tracers cut across the truck, one at window height, exploding glass from the windshield and back window, the second line punching through the doors and fenders and hammering the hood. The truck came to an abrupt halt as the weight of the dead driver pulled the steering wheel hard to the right.

"Going for weapons!" Lyons shouted to his partners as he sprinted to the truck, the two satchels of rockets beating at his sides. He jerked open a door, pulled out a dead man, saw a wounded man struggling to raise a pistol and he grabbed for the man's hair, but hooked his fingers in an eye instead. He jerked the screaming man out of the car and smashed a knee into his blood-spurting face.

He used the screaming man's auto-pistol to stop the screaming, then to shoot all the other dead and wounded in the head.

The attackers wore black web gear over sports coats and Lyons stripped off bandoliers of magazines and a pistol belt and took a short CAR assault rifle.

A grenade popped a distance behind him, the steel shrapnel pinging off the truck. He looked up to the roof of the building, and in the orange light of the fires saw forms moving. Aiming over the CAR's sights, he fired a wild spray of 5.56 mm slugs at the men on the roof.

One man staggered back. The other took cover. Bullets hammered the wrecked truck. Desperate, Lyons dropped the empty magazine of the CAR and tore another magazine from the gear of the dead man.

The man also wore a bandolier of 40 mm grenades, and Lyons searched for the man's weapon and found the single-shot launcher. He aimed at the roofline, released the safety and squeezed the trigger. White phosphorus splashed the guard post. A man screamed and ran wildly, appearing at the edge of the roof, then disappearing again, his screaming continuing.

Lyons loaded another shell and fired at the burning emplacement. High explosive sent chemical smoke clouding into the night. Reloading the 40 mm launcher and the CAR, and staggering with the weight of all the munitions he carried, Lyons lurched toward the center of the International's estate, pausing only to call back to his partners.

"Into it! Kill them all!"

35

Bodyguards shouted. Musicians packed their instruments. Blue-haired matrons cried. Aging public figures postured and waved their arms, directing their guards and aides.

The sound of panic had replaced music in the ballroom. Plainclothed soldiers of the International, their blazers replaced by flak vests and web gear, stood at the doors with rifles, waiting for the commands of their officers.

At the rear exit, Jon Gunther and a select group of soldiers guarded the leader of the Pan-American Reich, Miguel de la Unomundo. The young, immaculately groomed Unomundo smoked an imported cigarette. Ash fell on his tuxedo, and he flicked the gray dust away with his manicured fingers. Beside him, standing a head taller, Gunther monitored the fighting outside on a walkie-talkie.

"There are explosions on the perimeter. The volume of fire from the attackers already inside the defenses indicates a squad of men. It seems our men reacted too quickly to the threat and took many casualties before—"

"What about the helicopter?" Unomundo interrupted.

"The helipad is in flames. Your helicopter and the helicopters of several guests are—"

"Gone. That means limousines. Tell your men to assemble. We will take limousines out of here."

"Sir, there are enemy forces outside. We could drive into an ambush. It is better that we go upstairs into the communications center and wait until the security details eliminate the threat against us."

"Then let us go there. Immediately."

"And these others?" Gunther glanced to the crowd of panic-stricken guests.

"What of them?" Unomundo tapped out another cigarette and changed the subject. He turned away from Gunther and spoke to an aide. "I want our network in Washington to be alerted. I want to know who is responsible for this attack before the end of the business day tomorrow."

"Yes, sir. I will radio from the equipment upstairs and brief our—"

An explosion tore through the main doors of the ballroom, the double doors spinning, slicing through the crowd, hacking through torsos and severing legs as hundreds of fragments of wood and brass rained down on the screaming mass of guests. A line of tracers shot into the crowd, and elegant men and women fell, the elite of the capital panicking as indiscriminate slaughter sought them out.

Gunther holstered his pistol and picked up his commander and ran through the rear door, protecting Unomundo with his own body. The other security men crowded behind Gunther.

Another line of tracers scythed through the ballroom, the sound of the auto weapon lost in the screaming. A 40 mm grenade came through the smoking ruin of the entry and struck a bleeding, crawling fat man in the wide seat of his black formal trousers, his body disappearing in a spray of white fat tissue and pink meat.

In the next corridor, Gunther guided his commander up the stairs to the safety of the higher floors. He pointed to his most trustworthy men.

"No one passes here. You will stop anyone who comes."

They acknowledged with nods. Without questioning, they knew they would not survive a retreat. Gunther went back to the doors to the ballroom as guests crowded past him as they attempted to escape the terror.

A young man and his raven-haired date tried to follow their host up the stairs. Gunther's men shoved the couple back. When the young man protested and grabbed the nearest guard, the guard shot him and pushed him back into the stream of guests.

Gunther nodded approval to his men. At the double doors, he looked back into the ballroom. Under the soft light of the chandeliers, he saw a black-uniformed figure rush through the shattered entry. A squad automatic weapon flashed in his hands as he took cover in an alcove, firing bursts at everything that moved in the ballroom, cutting down the security men, guests, waiters, musicians indiscriminately.

Then another man entered and pointed a grenade launcher at the crowd jamming the rear exit.

In the instant before the man fired and Gunther dodged back to avoid the grenade, Gunther iden-

tified the man who wore casual slacks and sweatshirt issued from the estate's supply room.

Carl Lyons.

Leading an assault on the gathering of the fascist elite of the Americas.

Gunther knew the final confrontation had come.
He had brought that relentless machine of death
and destruction into the center of the International
and tried to mold that warrior to his service. He had
tried to use Lyons as his weapon. And failed.

Now he must kill him.

36

Lyons showed no mercy. The big guy fired and maneuvered, changed magazines and pirouetted, racing here and there on the blood-slick parquet dance floor, his battle-honed combat senses directing unerring bursts of bullets into debutantes and matrons, tuxedos and ties.

This merciless vendetta had its origins in years of frustration, the unending chase of transnational responsibility from action to action. Every atrocity had its perpetrators, those who actually executed the crimes and those who ordered the crimes. Able Team had succeeded in hitting the gunmen and local gangsters, but never before, not until this night, not until they had been reunited by chance within the concentric circles of security and charged into the high-society gaiety of the capital elite, not until they pointed their weapons at bankers and debutantes and corporate executives did they actually get the opportunity to execute the monsters who directed the International's terror.

Moving faster as he expended ammunition, Lyons zigzagged across the dance floor in a fox-trot of mayhem, a tap dance of murder, a waltz of payback. But his short-barreled Colt Commando only played rock and roll. He swung it like a conductor's baton, a metronome of death, setting the rhythm of slaughter, spraying staccato sixteenth notes of 5.5 mm oblivion.

The river of flesh—costumed in the New York and London and Paris styles of the jet-set corporate elite—suddenly wore the unfashionable colors of massacre, the red of blood, the gray of splashed brains and the white of shattered bones.

The three fearless, battle-hardened warriors of Able Team slashed their way through the crowd, every step through the gore and corsages closing the distance between them and their target:

Unomundo.

Intermittent pistol and submachine gun fire came from the few bodyguards intermixed with the mob. Gadgets fired from the hip at the moving gunmen, using the armor-piercing slugs from his M 249 to slice through the people blocking his line of fire, the lines of slugs and tracers like a laser through soggy macaroni salad.

But the rifle fire from the International soldiers staging a delaying action delayed Able Team. Lyons went flat in the blood as slugs from the CARs of the security men zipped past. Three tux-clad bodies protected Lyons as he snapped out the tube of another LAW rocket. Before firing, he took the time to check the load of his 40 mm grenade launcher—high explosive and shrapnel.

Lyons fired the LAW rocket at the rear exit, the rocket flashing across the twenty yards of dance floor. The explosion left the walls dripping gore and plastered with fragments of brocade and silk. A bow tie fluttered throught the air like a butterfly.

Then Lyons signaled to his partners and rushed. Lines of 5.56 mm slugs converged on his goal, and suddenly the few soldiers and bodyguards no longer existed.

Slipping and sliding, Lyons slammed against the wall.

As he pushed to the stairs, a grenade bounced down. He dropped down into the dead and dying ballroom debris and the blast sent steel-wire razors slicing past. He crabbed back to the entry as another grenade popped.

Gadgets and Blancanales crouched on each side of the entry. Smoke rose from the hot barrels of their M-249 machine guns.

"The goons went up those stairs."

Blancanales glanced to the ceiling of the ballroom. "This building's about six stories. Means there's several floors up above us."

"I saw microwave antennas on the roof," Gadgets added. "They must have offices and what all—"

"And they got a flat roof," Lyons interrupted. "Means they could bring in a helicopter to get the slime out of here. We either waste this entire building, right away, or we go up there and find him."

"Office to office?" Gadgets shook his head. "Forget that. You know where he is, I'll go get him, but I won't go looking."

"Negative on a search," Blancanales added.

"You bring anything that could take down this building?"

"Like a backpack nuke?" Gadgets asked. "There is a limit, you know. I'll look around, but I doubt if they stockpile C-4 in the kitchen."

"Do it. But trade with me first. Take this Commando and give me your Black Beauty and the ammo. I'll go up to the roof and stop the helicopter."

In seconds, Lyons had exchanged weapons and bandoliers. He kept only one of the LAW rockets, slinging the fiberglass launch tube over his bulky mags of linked cartridges.

"And take your radio!" Gadget said.

"You brought one for me?" Lyons asked.

"We figured you'd want to catch up on the baseball scores."

And Lyons moved. He knew there had to be another way up to the higher floors. Chandeliers. Spotlights. That meant an attic space above the domed ceiling of the ballroom.

Rushing to the stage, Lyons found the stage manager's booth. Levers and switches controlled the stage area and the lighting of the ballroom. Another position controlled the public-address system and the surrounding speakers. Finally, he saw the locked door marked Electrical Access.

Shooting out the lock, he went up the narrow spiral stairs at a run. He came to a catwalk leading over the arched structural members of the ballroom dome. In the half-light cast by the work

lights, he scanned the area. He saw air-conditioning
ducts. And a door.

The door led to another spiral stairway, this
stairway rising through columns of duct work.
Lyons continued upward through the duct shaft.
Around him, he heard the whirring of motors.
Then he reached a platform and another door.

Outside, he heard voices, and in the distance,
shooting. Switching off the worklights, he waited,
listening. Men shouted to one another. He heard
footsteps. His right hand holding the pistol grip of
the slung M 249, he eased the door open with his
left hand.

Lyons saw landing lights flashing. Men with
weapons stood at the edge of the roof, watching the
estate grounds. He slipped out the door and stood
against the air-conditioner housing. In the shadows, he watched a squad leader go from man to
man. The officer checked with two men manning a
machine gun in a fixed emplacement. Then the officer spoke into a walkie-talkie.

On one side of the building, flames rose from the
burning helicopters and vehicles. The night glowed
orange. Swirls of acrid smoke from burning tires
and plastic made men cough.

An explosion boomed from the perimeter, the
darkness white for an instant. The security men
scanned that area with night-vision binoculars, but
no one fired or changed positions.

Then, in the distance, Lyons heard helicopters,
the rotor throb approaching fast. He saw no lights
or aircraft until the helicopters circled. The fire-

light revealed helicopters with blue and white commercial painting and corporate insignia.

But a machine gun flashed from the side door of one chopper, and as the corporate-shuttle helicopter completed a slow orbit of the estate, the door gunner fired wildly into the woods outside the landscaped grounds. The other helicopter came in for a slow landing.

Too slow, Lyons thought. Gadgets had downed one helicopter with machine gun fire, and Lyons had hit another one with a rocket. Why did the pilots now expose their aircraft to the groundfire of the attackers?

To test the response of the attackers, Lyons realized. If the attackers hit one of the helicopters, they knew the attackers still had men outside the main building.

Why would the officers of the International be willing to sacrifice a helicopter and crew to learn the positions of the enemy?

The second helicopter hovered above the roof for almost a minute, then finally touched down. Men with rifles jumped out the side doors. An officer directed the soldiers to positions along the roof.

Rotors roaring, the gunship came in and circled the building, the door gunner shooting shadows and trees with bursts of 7.62 mm NATO. Every orbit of the building risked a rocket or machine gun fire from the enemies attacking the estate.

Lyons guessed the reason for the extraordinary risk. He let the M 249 hang by its sling and slipped off the LAW rocket. He crouched in a space be-

tween two housings, glanced back to confirm no
obstructions behind him and held the LAW tube
ready.

Knotted around one man in a tuxedo, a group of
men rushed from a stairwell housing. Gunther led
the group. Lyons knew who they protected.

Unomundo.

Lyons pulled out the launcher's tube and waited.
The group of men escorted Unomundo to the helicopter, and the leader of the International climbed
through the side door. Two men accompanied him.
But not Gunther.

Gunther shouted to his officers. Every man
around the roof fired down at the grounds of the
estate, pistols, submachine guns, rifles, machine
guns—every weapon at once. The moment was
now! The helicopter lifted away and Lyons fired.

The rocket punched through the Plexiglas windshield and gutted the helicopter in a micro-second,
the Plexiglas and side doors exploding outward, the
shell of destroyed helicopter remaining airborne
only an instant before falling straight down to the
roof. The fuel exploded on impact, enveloping men
in the fireball, tongues of flaming fuel spraying
everywhere.

For a moment, all motion stopped, every man on
the rooftop turning toward the flaming crash. But
Gunther had seen the rocket flash, and he rushed
toward Lyons.

Lyons dropped the spent tube and brought up the
M 249, triggering a burst as the barrel went on target, a line of tracers cutting through one of Gunth-

er's legs but not stopping him. The hulking, powerful man continued his rush on adrenaline, the line of tracers continuing upward, tearing through his abdomen, still not stopping him. Lyons held back the trigger as Gunther hurtled toward him, the line of tracers passing throught the already dead man's chest until the high-velocity slugs tore through his spine and severed the reflexive drive to kill.

The body of Jon Gunther came to a sliding stop in front of Lyons and he swept the muzzle of the M 249 from one side to the other, soldiers of the International dying, falling back off the roof, men trying to react to the surprise and confusion, dying as they raised their weapons.

Bullets slammed into the air-conditioning housing, and Lyons threw open the door leading to the duct shaft and retreated. He locked the door, and as bullets slammed into it and the housing, he jammed a white phosphorus round between the knob and the doorframe, then ran down the stairs.

But when the gunmen shot through the lock, the bullets did not detonate the cartridge. Bullets hammered around Lyons as he ran down the steel steps, four at a time. A grenade exploded above him. He ran the last few steps and pushed aside the door to the ballroom attic.

As he shoved the door closed, another grenade exploded, the shock to the door numbing his hands. He heard feet running down the steel stairs. This time he waited at the door, the M 249 level. With his left hand, he keyed his hand-radio:

"I killed him. I killed Unomundo. Prepare to get out of here."

"All right! Second the motion!" came back the reply from Gadgets.

The pursuing men prepped the door with rifle fire, then kicked it aside. Lyons unleashed an entire magazine.

No one pursued him as he ran down the next spiral to the ballroom stage.

His partners saw him and they ran. Weapons flashing, they disappeared into the night.

Mack Bolan's

PHOENIX FORCE

by Gar Wilson

Schooled in guerrilla warfare, equipped with all the latest lethal hardware, Phoenix Force battles the powers of darkness in an endless crusade for freedom, justice and the rights of the individual. Follow the adventures of one of the legends of the genre. Phoenix Force is the free world's foreign legion!

"Gar Wilson is excellent! Raw action attacks the reader on every page."

—*Don Pendleton*

Phoenix Force titles are available wherever paperbacks are sold.

GOLD EAGLE

DON PENDLETON'S EXECUTIONER
MACK BOLAN

Sergeant Mercy in Nam…The Executioner in the Mafia Wars…Colonel John Phoenix in the Terrorist Wars…Now Mack Bolan fights his loneliest war! You've never read writing like this before. By fire and maneuver, Bolan will rack up hell in a world shock-tilted by terror. He wages unsanctioned war—everywhere!

GOLD
EAGLE

4 FREE BOOKS
1 FREE GIFT
NO RISK
NO OBLIGATION
NO KIDDING

SPECIAL LIMITED-TIME OFFER

Mail to **Gold Eagle Reader Service**

In the U.S.
2504 West Southern Ave.
Tempe, AZ 85282

In Canada
P.O. Box 2800, Station A
5170 Yonge St.,
Willowdale, Ont. M2N 6J3

YEAH! Rush me 4 free Gold Eagle novels and my free mystery bonus. Then send me 6 brand-new novels every other month as they come off the presses. Bill me at the low price of $2.25 each— a 10% saving off the retail price. There are no shipping, handling or other hidden costs. There is no minimum number of books I must buy. I can always return a shipment and cancel at any time. Even if I never buy another book from Gold Eagle, the 4 free novels and the mystery bonus are mine to keep forever.

Name _____ (PLEASE PRINT)

Address _____ Apt. No. _____

City _____ State/Prov. _____ Zip/Postal Code _____

Signature (If under 18, parent or guardian must sign)

This offer is limited to one order per household and not valid to present subscribers. Price is subject to change.

166-BPM-BPGE   NO–SUB–1